To Bella & Beth
From
loykey & lillybit
04.07.10.

Alice and Alfie
and the
magic windmill

written and illustrated by

Loykey & Lillybit

A CIP record for this book
is available from the British Library

ISBN 978-0-956233-30-1

Alice and *Alfie* are two
rag dolls who belong to a
little girl called Nichole.
One summer her family
go on holiday to France
to a beautiful windmill.
On their return to
England the rag dolls are
accidentally left behind
and magically come alive
and this is where their
journey begins..............

CONTENTS

Alice and *Alfie*

CONTENTS

Alice and *Alfie*

Alice and *Alfie*
and the Magic Windmill

There was once a little girl called Nichole, she lived with her mummy and daddy in a little village in Sussex. This story begins when her mummy and daddy said to her at dinner that their holiday this year was going to be in France. She was so excited, she ran upstairs and lay on the bed with her best friends *Alice* and *Alfie* her rag dolls. Nichole told them they were going on holiday to France.

Nichole went back downstairs and as she left the room *Alice* and *Alfie,* magically came alive, but this only happened when Nichole and her mummy and daddy were not around. They jumped up and down and got very excited. Suddenly, they heard Nichole coming back up the stairs and they fell to the floor and became rag dolls once again.

The holiday came round so quickly. The cases were
packed, the car was loaded and the rag dolls were
packed with their heads peeking out of Nichole's
rucksack in the back of the car. So off they went.

Nichole and her family all went on a big ship on the sea. It was lovely. Soon they were in France where they drove through a big forest. At the end of the forest there was a clearing and there in front of them was the most beautiful windmill. Nichole's mummy said to her, "This is where we are staying for our holiday." The rag dolls *Alice* and *Alfie* could see the windmill and their faces lit up with joy for they knew that no one else could see them.

Nichole jumped out of the car and ran up to the windmill. It looked so big, but to her it was magical with its big hands turning in the wind. She went inside with her mummy and daddy. The rooms downstairs were beautiful where there was a lounge and kitchen. Nichole went upstairs where she found two bedrooms and a bathroom. Nichole chose her bedroom and her mummy and daddy had the other room.

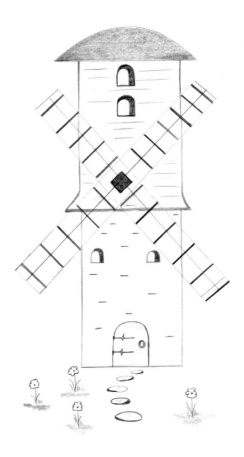

Nichole went to the window and watched the hands of the windmill going round; it was lovely to see. She could also see the river and she watched the ducks with their ducklings on the water and could not wait to go down to see them. As she left the room *Alice* and *Alfie* came alive once again. They went to the window and could not believe their eyes. They saw the water and the ducks and they danced round and round saying what a jolly holiday this was going to be. Just at that moment the door handle turned. It was Nichole's mummy, so *Alice* and *Alfie* dropped to the floor.

Nichole's mummy picked up the rag dolls and muttered to herself, "Nichole is so untidy leaving her toys everywhere." She looked out of the open window and called to her, "I have made some lunch. It is time to come in."

As Nichole's mummy left the room *Alice* and *Alfie* jumped up and went back to the window. They spotted a ladder up the side of the window. *Alice* looked at *Alfie* and said, "Shall we?" and down they went.

Alice and *Alfie* went straight to the ducks and
ducklings. Nichole had left some bread on the side
of the river so they carried on feeding the ducklings.
The two rag dolls just sat there magically drawn to the
windmill. *Alice* said to *Alfie*, "I would love to live
here forever."

The week of the holiday was fantastic and the rag dolls were taken everywhere with Nichole. They went on walks through the woods where they saw the wood pigeons and owls and they were also taken fishing where Nichole's daddy caught some fish with a rod and line. The week went by so quickly. Every night Nichole would put the rag dolls to bed in a little box in the corner of her bedroom and cover them over with a blanket before she went to sleep.

The day arrived to go home and Nichole's daddy was rushing around as the family were late getting up and they had to get back to the ship on time. Nichole was still asleep when her mummy came into the bedroom. Mummy said, "Go to the bathroom and wash and I will pack your things." As Nichole washed, her mummy knocked on the door and said, "I will meet you downstairs." Nichole had some breakfast and then daddy said, "We must leave now I have packed the car." Nichole said goodbye to the windmill that had been so magical to her and said, "We will be back some day." And they all climbed into the car and began the journey home.

When they arrived home Nichole started to unpack her case. Suddenly she started crying and shouting and her mummy rushed upstairs to see what had happened.
Mummy said, "What is wrong, Nichole?
Nichole answered, "*Alice* and *Alfie* are not in my case, where are they?"
Mummy asked her "When did you last have them?"
"I put them to bed in the corner of the bedroom in the windmill." Nichole replied.
 "I did not see them there, I am sorry." Mummy said, "I do not know what to say. We will have to go shopping and buy you some more rag dolls."
But Nichole sobbed, "They are special to me; can we go back?"
Mummy replied, "No I'm sorry, Nichole. We can't."

Nichole cried all night and in the early hours she saw the moon was shining down onto the house. Nichole looked out of the window and the moon said to her, "Don't worry, Nichole. *Alice* and *Alfie* will be alright. I'll keep watch over them." Nichole thanked the moon and went off to sleep and dreamt about her rag dolls at the magic windmill.

M<small>eanwhile</small>.........

back at the windmill *Alice* and *Alfie* suddenly
came alive and this is where their journey began.....

"Oh, *Alfie*, it would be lovely to stay here forever."

Alice and *Alfie* Best Friends

Alice and *Alfie* came alive as they heard the car
going up the road away from the windmill. They ran
to the window and saw Nichole and her mummy and
daddy disappear into the distance. At that moment their
little hearts sank and they could not imagine what life
was going to be like not having Nichole with them.

Alice said to *Alfie*, "They have left us and we are all alone,"

Alfie said, "Don't worry we will be alright," and just at that moment they heard the front door open. They looked down the staircase and saw a little old man with a white short beard and a small black cotton hat. They quickly ran back to the bedroom and sat very still on the windowsill. The old man, whose name was Jacques, came into the bedroom and put his suitcase on the bed. He was the owner of the windmill and he had rented it out to Nichole's mummy and daddy.

Jacques saw the rag dolls on the windowsill. He picked them up and said to himself, "What lovely toys." He realised that Nichole and her mummy and daddy had left them behind. He put them back on the windowsill and went downstairs to get some dinner.

As Jacques walked downstairs, *Alice* and *Alfie* came alive. They looked out of the window and spotted some kittens running around by the water. Jacques had bought them back with him to try and keep the mice away. All of a sudden two little mice came running into the bedroom. They saw *Alice* and *Alfie* and started shouting, "Please help us."

Alice said, "Quick, jump into our pockets." *Alice* lay down and *Alfie* lay in front of her and they told the mice to keep very still. The kittens ran into the bedroom but could not find the mice, so they scurried downstairs and sat in front of the large log fire that Jacques had lit. He sat there and ate his dinner and the kittens had their milk.

Alice took the mice out of her pocket and said to *Alfie*, "We will have to hide them somewhere." They decided the best place was in the box that Nichole used to put them in at night. The mice thanked them for what they had done and then they said that when Jacques went out they would show *Alice* and *Alfie* the windmill and the woods.

That night after everyone had gone to bed, the two rag dolls sat at the window when all of a sudden the moon floated down. To their amazement the moon spoke to them, saying, "Nichole sends her love to you both and says she will be back for you one day."

The next morning when *Alice* and *Alfie* awoke they
heard the kittens playing in the garden and saw Jacques
go off to town to do some shopping.
Alice said, "Lets go down and play. I should like
to take the mice with us." The mice sat up and said,
"What!...what!... They will eat us!"
Alice replied, "No they won't. We will all be friends,"
and so they all climbed down the ladder at the side of the
window and went off to join the kittens.

The rag dolls sat and played with the kittens and *Alice* said, "I have brought some new friends for you to play with," and the kittens said, "Where?...where?... Do show us."

Alice took the mice out of her pocket and the mice said, "Don't eat us, please don't eat us." The kittens laughed and replied, "We only chase mice because we want to play with them," and so they all became good friends.

Alice said to *Alfie,* "I can't believe it we have made some friends already."   That night when they went to bed the moon shone down and said to them, "Nichole sends her love and hopes you have lots of fun on your adventures."   The moon then drifted away and they both fell fast asleep.

Alice and *Alfie*

The Magic of the Windmill

The next morning Jacques the windmill keeper got up really early and fed the ducks and kittens and then had his breakfast. After he had eaten he went round the side of the windmill where there was a big barn.

Suddenly there was a loud grinding sound that woke *Alice* and *Alfie.* The rag dolls looked out of the window and to their amazement the four big sails of the windmill came rushing past. They could not believe what they were seeing. *Alice* said to *Alfie,* "It must be a magic windmill." They sat on the windowsill and watched the hands going round and round in the wind.

Alice and *Alfie* wanted to have a closer look and crept downstairs. At the end of the kitchen they saw a door which was half open. They peeked through the door and they could see the windmill machinery going round and round. The rag dolls saw Jacques in the corner putting corn grain onto a big stone and then another larger stone came down on top grinding away. *Alice* and *Alfie* realised the windmill sails were making the stones go round to grind the grain which produced the flour.

Alice said to *Alfie,* "I wonder what that powder is for." They watched Jacques put the powder into bags, around which he tied a piece of string, to stop it spilling out. He put the sacks into the back of his van. *Alice* said, "Let's see where he goes." Just before Jacques drove off they ran and jumped into the back of the van. At the back of the sacks they spotted a large old bucket and they quickly jumped in.

Jacques drove through the woods and up and down the hills until he reached a little village where he stopped. It was right outside a small shop with a sign outside saying BAKERY. *Alice* and *Alfie* jumped out of the van and ran up the side of the shop and peered in through a doorway.

Inside the doorway they stared with amazement. The baker said to Jacques, "Thank you for the flour. Would you like to watch me make the bread?" *Alice* and *Alfie* watched the baker make the bread and put it into the oven. It smelt absolutely lovely. Jacques said, "I must be off now, I have to get back to the windmill to make some more flour." The rag dolls ran to the van and quickly jumped back into the bucket. The baker came out with Jacques and said, "Thank you, Jacques, for the lovely flour." The baker also gave him two loaves of bread and some cakes.

When they got back the sails on the windmill had stopped. *Alice* said to *Alfie*, "It is a magic windmill and it will do it all again tomorrow."

That night they lay on the windowsill and went to sleep. All of a sudden there was a tap on the window. It was the moon and he said goodnight to the rag dolls and told them Nichole sent her love. Then the Moon puffed out his cheeks and blew and blew and the sails on the windmill went round and round as the two rag dolls drifted off to sleep.

"Alfie, I would like to bake some cakes"

Alice and *Alfie* Go Camping

Jacques the windmill keeper was down in the kitchen making his breakfast. *Alice* and *Alfie* heard him talking on the phone saying he was going to his brother's for the weekend. *Alice* said, "We will be on our own for two or three days. What shall we do?" *Alfie* replied, "Down in the barn I saw a small tent hanging up. We could go camping." *Alice* said, "Oh, can we? Please, please, please let us go." So they waited until Jacques' van had left, then they went down to the barn and there it was, a small tent hanging up. They took it down and carefully put it into a small bag that they found on the floor.

Alfie went back into the windmill and put some water
and food into a bag and their journey began.
They walked along the side of the river and the
butterflies flew with them and kept them amused for
ages. They came to an old bridge where they sat
and watched the fish swimming in the water. They
carried on down the riverbank and they saw a beautiful
waterfall that had a little sandy beach at the end.
Alfie said, "I'm going for a paddle in the water."
Alice followed.

The rag dolls splashed each other with water and got soaking wet and really enjoyed themselves. Afterwards they sat on the grass and dried themselves off. *Alice* said, "Look at the sun going down over the hill. Can we pitch the tent here tonight, *Alfie?* It is so lovely." "OK *Alice* let us do that," answered *Alfie.*

The two rag dolls had fun and games putting up the tent. It was upside down, inside out. They just could not get it right. They just sat there looking at the tangled tent then Mr. Frank the Owl flew down and said, "I see you are having problems. I have seen all this before," and then he showed them how to put up the tent. They were so grateful, they said, "Would you like some food and water?"

Mr. Frank replied, "Thank you." They sat and ate the food and afterwards he flew off into the woods singing ta-wit-ta-woo. The owl returned with some lovely red plums to thank them for the food.

At that moment a tiny little deer came out of the woods. They only had water left but he was very grateful and he said, "I will stay with you all night along with the owl and keep you both safe." And with that they all went off to sleep.

The next morning *Alice* and *Alfie* woke up to find the owl and the deer had gone. They packed up their tent and went on their way following the river. In the distance they saw a castle. It was beautiful and when they were close they could see that the river went all the way round. They also saw that there was no bridge to cross the water.

Alice said to *Alfie*, "I would love to go and see the castle,"
Alfie replied, "There is no way of getting to the other side, not even a boat."

Just then from the top of the castle a swan flew down and landed next to them. "Do you wish to see the castle?" he said.
"Oh, yes please," said *Alice*.
"Jump on my back then and I will fly you to the castle." With that they went up, up and away.

The swan flew gracefully over the castle walls and landed in the courtyard of the castle. He said to them, "It is a magical castle. Just have fun and I will return later to take you back across the water." *Alice* and *Alfie* thanked him and set off to explore.

The rag dolls walked up a wide stone staircase to a huge old wooden door. *Alfie* opened it slowly and they walked through into a big hall. At the end of the hall there were some puppets dressed as clowns. They were dancing to some music that was being played by two cats and their kittens. The cats were playing the drums and the kittens were playing whistle flutes. They asked *Alice* and *Alfie* to join in, *Alice* said, "We would love to." and they danced and danced and danced.

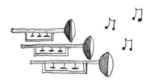

After a while dancing, the rag dolls sat down on a
bench. They were so worn out. Then all of a sudden
some trumpets blew and the kittens shouted, "It's the
PRINCE." The prince entered and sat down at the top
of a long table. The rag dolls noticed that he looked
just the same as the wood the table was made of. He
told *Alice* and *Alfie* that he was indeed made out of
wood – he was the wooden prince. He said, "Where
do you come from?" They told him about the windmill
and he said, "That sounds magical. I would love to
see this windmill, but because I am made out of wood,
I cannot go outside as my joints will rot in the wet and
rain and so I stay indoors with all my friends."

43

The prince invited the rag dolls to eat with him and as they ate he said, "Tell me more about your travels." *Alice* and *Alfie* told him all about Nichole and about all their adventures. They talked for a long time until it was dark outside. The wooden prince said they could stay the night and showed them to their bedroom. *Alice* thanked him and they both fell fast asleep on a huge bed.

Alice and *Alfie* were woken soon after by a tapping sound on the window. The rag dolls looked out to see a glowing light. It was the moon and he said Jacques was on his way home and they must leave. The moon told them, "Close your eyes and make a wish, count to three and twitch your noses." In no time at all they were back at the windmill. *Alfie* quickly put the tent into the barn and rushed upstairs with *Alice*. They had just climbed onto the windowsill as Jacques turned up in the van. "That was close," said the moon. "Nichole says goodnight. God bless and sleep well."

"*Alice*, we must go camping again. What fun!"

Alice and *Alfie*

The Day the Snow Came

It was the first cold day of December and *Alice* and *Alfie* woke to hear Jacques downstairs talking to someone. It was his friend Francois who had come to stay. Jacques said to him, "It is going to snow. I have a feeling in my bones." he said.

François replied, "I think you are right. We will have to get lots of logs in for the fire I will go and get the logs while you cook the breakfast."

Alice said to *Alfie*, "Do you know what they are talking about? What do they mean by snow?" *Alfie* was confused, "Perhaps it is a kind of wind." That day it got colder and colder and Jacques lit a big log fire. The heat from the fire gradually crept upstairs where *Alice* and *Alfie* were sitting snugly on the landing. They heard Jacques say to Francois, "You can have my room as it is warmer," and so Francois picked up his cases and went upstairs.

Alice and *Alfie* ran to the bedroom window and lay very still as they always did. Francois put his clothes in the cupboard and as he turned he saw the toys on the windowsill and picked them up saying, "It is going to snow you know." He put them back on the sill and went downstairs.

Alice and *Alfie* jumped up and *Alice* said, "It is going to snow but what is snow?" Just then they looked out of the window and they were amazed at the white fluffy stuff falling to the ground. They heard Jacques shout to Francois. "There, I told you. It's snowing." *Alice* said, "That's snow! Isn't it beautiful?"

That afternoon the snow fell more and more and *Alice* said, "It is getting deeper and deeper." They looked through the window and saw Jacques and Francois go out of the back door. The two rag dolls saw them get handfuls of snow and squeeze them in their hands, making a ball, and then start throwing them at each other. After a while they came back in and sat by the big log fire to warm.

Alice said, "I would love to do that."
Alfie replied, "Yes, let's." So they climbed down the ladder at the side of the window. The snow was still falling. They both thought it was magical and they started making snowballs too and threw them at each other.

After a while they got so cold they decided to go into the barn where it was warmer. *Alfie* said, "Look what is hanging up on the wall." It was a seat with a cord and a handle and some metal tracks. *Alice* said "Perhaps you can pull me on it in the snow?" *Alfie* pulled it outside and they went round to the back of the barn so Jacques and Francois could not see them.

There was a little slope down to the riverbank, they both sat on the sledge and to their amazement they started to move. They went up and down on the little sledge all afternoon. It was brilliant. Later, as they were coming back up the hill they saw a large heap of snow in the distance. It was quite tall and it seemed to have a head, so they trudged over to it and as they walked around to the front *Alice* said, "What is it?"

It had a carrot for a nose, and two large lumps of coal for eyes and a woollen scarf and hat. *Alfie* said, "It is made of snow and it is a man so we shall call him Mr. Snowman."

He looked so sad and so *Alice* tickled the snowman's tummy and all of a sudden he came alive. *Alfie* said, "What is your name?" and the snowman replied, "I am Mr. Snowman."
Alice said, "Wow! We guessed his name."

The snowman told them he could not move. *Alice* was upset and sad. She said, "*Alfie*, can we take him back to our bedroom?" The snowman, shouted "No, no, no, if you take me back indoors I will melt and another year will have gone."

"Every year I get built and every year as it gets warmer I melt and disappear."

Alice said, "We will come and see you every day." and the snowman said thank you to them both.

The rag dolls both went to see Mr. Snowman every day, but little by little they saw that he was melting away. One day *Alice* and *Alfie* felt it was a lot warmer and the snow had started to melt. As they turned the corner they saw that the snowman had disappeared and only the carrot, the coal and the hat and scarf remained on the ground. *Alice* cried and cried and cried but *Alfie* said, "Don't cry *Alice*, he will be back again next year."

It was getting dark so they went back to the windmill and fell fast asleep. Shortly afterwards there was a tap on the window which woke them up. As the rag dolls looked up they saw that the moon was smiling down on them. For the first time the moon had bought a friend. It was a bright sparkling star, which they had never seen before.

 The moon told them, "The bright sparkling star is Nichole's own star and she has a message for you that says, "I love you both very much." The star twinkled away into the distance as *Alice* and *Alfie* went off to sleep with their dreams.

"Alfie, I do hope Mr. Snowman is back next year."

Alice and *Alfie*

Christmas Comes but Once a Year

Alice was awoken by lots of talking downstairs. She woke *Alfie* and they crept to the top of the stairs. They could see Jacques and Francois sitting at the table. In the doorway were Jacques's brother and his wife and their two children. Jacques had invited them all for Christmas. *Alice* and *Alfie* did not know what Christmas was but they were about to find out.

The children were called Melanie and Jerome. Jacques said there was a small room at the end of the kitchen and he would sleep in there. Francois was going home to his family for Christmas, so he said that Jacques's brother's family could have the two bedrooms upstairs.

Melanie and Jerome ran upstairs to find their bedroom.
The rag dolls had to drop to the floor at the doorway as
they had no time to get to the windowsill. The children
nearly tripped over them as they put their cases on the
bed. Melanie and Jerome picked up the rag dolls. The
children chose one each and laid them on their beds and
then they ran back downstairs.

Jacques went to the village to buy more food for the Christmas holiday. The family went outside to look at the windmill. Jerome went into the mill where he found a big wheel. Melanie said, "I don't think you should touch that, " but being a boy, of course he did. Jerome turned the wheel very slowly and all of a sudden the windmill's sails began to move. Jerome and Melanie ran outside and said to their mummy and daddy, "Look it's magic. The hands are moving." By this time *Alice* and *Alfie* were on the windowsill. They knew the windmill's secret but could not tell the children.

Jacques returned with the food for Christmas and in the back of his van was a big fir tree. They put it up in the lounge and put lights, tinsel and balls on it with chocolate toys. That evening after dinner, Jacques and the family went for a walk down to the river.

Alice and *Alfie* crept downstairs. To their joy they found the magical tree. They sat down in front of the log fire and stared at the pretty tree in amazement. After a while they both fell fast asleep in front of the log fire and were still there when the door opened and the family arrived back. *Alice* and *Alfie* were fast asleep and Jerome and Melanie could not understand how they had got there. However, they decided to leave them by the fire as they looked so peaceful.

The next morning there was a loud knock on the door which woke *Alice* and *Alfie*. Jacques went and opened the door and there was the postman with a large sack. He said, "Lots of post today for you Jacques." Jacques replied, "Yes, I have my family staying with me."

The postman wished him a Merry Christmas but *Alice* and *Alfie* still did not know what Christmas was.

All day the rag dolls watched the family baking cakes and getting food ready for Christmas Day. Jerome said, "I cannot wait for tomorrow, I am going to get up really early,"
 "I am too." Melanie replied.

Jerome told his mummy and daddy that they were going to bed so they could wake up really early. They picked up the rag dolls and went to their room where they laid *Alice* and *Alfie* on their beds and fell fast asleep.

After a while *Alfie* and *Alice* gently crept out of
bed and went and sat on the windowsill. They saw
the magical stars shining in the sky with one larger
star shining over the windmill. All of a sudden, far
away over the hills, they saw a sledge like thing. It
was just like the one they played with in the snow but
a lot bigger. It had six large reindeer pulling it with a
smiling man in a red coat and a white beard riding on
the back.

Alice said to *Alfie*, "How can it fly?" Then before
Alfie could reply the sleigh had landed on the roof of
the windmill.

The rag dolls rushed downstairs and to their surprise the red coated old man was laying presents around the tree. *Alfie* said, "Hello, who are you?"
The man replied, "Ho, Ho, Ho, rag dolls that can talk! I'm Father Christmas. I can't remember making you two. You must be very special."

"Wait a minute" he said, "Are your names *Alice* and *Alfie*?" They both nodded and said, "yes" together. "I have a special present for you; I will put it next to the other presents." He told them. "I must go now." And to their amazement he walked over to the chimney and flew up it so fast that as they looked out of the window he was already back on his sleigh and shouting "Ho, Ho, Ho and away we go," and flying off into the distance. The rag dolls rushed back upstairs and got into bed.

The next morning they heard the sound of children shouting, "It's just what I wanted, what lovely toys." Mummy, daddy and Jacques sat round the tree and opened their presents. Soon all the presents had been opened except one. Jacques picked up the present and read the tag, "It reads, for *Alice* and *Alfie* the rag dolls, all my love Nichole." Jacques told the children to go and get the rag dolls from their bedroom and they sat them in front of the fireplace and then they opened the present. It was a poem that Nichole had written and put into a frame it read:

CHRISTMAS LUNCH

WINDMILL SOUP

ROAST TURKEY AND VEG FROM THE MAGIC GARDEN

MINCE PIES AND WINDMILL DELIGHTS

CHOCOLATES OFF THE TREE......

Alice and *Alfie* Happy Christmas,
I miss you so much,
Keep huddled together,
Keep warm and dry,
I will be back some day,
So do not cry.
Thinking of the lovely time we spent together,
At the windmill with sunny weather,
My life is empty without you two,
One day I will come to collect you.
Love Nichole xx

The children had a lovely Christmas. They put the rag dolls to bed with the poem between them. That night the moon shone bright. He said, "*Alice* and *Alfie*, Nichole says goodnight and don't let the bed bugs bite."

Alice and *Alfie*
The Country Fair and Sports Day

One day there was a knock at the door and Jacques opened it. It was the local vicar. Jacques said, "Come in," and they sat and chatted at the table in the kitchen. The vicar told Jacques that in two weeks time it was the village fair and sports day and he asked Jacques if he could help. Jacques always helped every year and said he would think of some things he could do and then get in touch with him.

Alice and *Alfie* were at the top of the stairs and heard what was said. *Alice* said, "It sounds exciting. I hope we can go."

Alfie said, "There will be lots of children and we will have to be very careful."

The two weeks passed quickly and when the day came and Jacques loaded his van with lots of things that he had been making in the barn. *Alice* and *Alfie* climbed down the ladder by the side of the window and ran to the van and jumped into the bucket in the corner.

Jacques drove through the woods where two pigeons were following the van going coo, coo. *Alice* waved to them and they flew down and landed in the back of the van. *Alice* and *Alfie* jumped out of the bucket and said, "Hello." The birds said coo, coo. *Alice* said to them, "We are going to the village fair. Is that where you are going?" The birds replied that no, they couldn't go to the fair because if they went they could be shot and that was why they were going to stay in the woods all day.

Jacques drove right up to the village green. There was a fun fair and music was playing. It was a band of boys and girls playing drums, flutes and trumpets. *Alice* said to *Alfie*, "What a lovely sound." The van came to a halt and Jacques started unloading the stall that he had built. He had painted it in lots of lovely colours and at the far end there was a big sign saying Coconut Shy. He put up wooden posts and bales of straw all the way round. He had two buckets of wooden balls that he had made and he stood them at the front of the stall.

Jacques went back to the van to pick up the last bucket, but put it down quickly as it had a hole in the bottom. He decided to use the old bucket he had at the back of the van, the one that had had *Alice* and *Alfie* in it. They were lucky as he didn't see them. Jacques needed the empty bucket to collect all the balls that would be lying around. *Alice* said, "We can't stay in here," so when nobody was looking they jumped out and ran around the back of the straw bales. All of a sudden there was a loud blast of trumpets and everybody knew the mayor had arrived for the grand opening.

"LET THIS FAIR BE OPEN" announced the mayor and the crowds came running in. They were queueing up at Jacques' stall and were paying for six wooden balls and within moments balls were being thrown everywhere. *Alice* popped her head up and was nearly hit by a wooden ball. *Alfie* said it was too dangerous to stay there and they should move to another stall. They crept around the back of the stalls until they found the gun shooting range. People were trying to knock down packets of sweets and toys with pellets fired from rifles.

The rag dolls watched from behind the stall and once again nearly got hit, this time by wooden pellets. *Alfie* said to *Alice,* "Let's find somewhere much safer."

Alice looked across the field and in the middle of the fair was an area with straw bales all the way round the edge. It was called the arena. It was the sports day area. There were little girls and boys playing a game called the egg and spoon race. They had to run with an egg on a spoon without letting it fall off. Across the way mummies and daddies were doing the sack race. They were trying to run and jump in sacks which the rag dolls thought very funny.

Alice and *Alfie* were hiding behind two of the straw
bales when a pony and trap went past. At the back of
the trap there was a square box and blankets and hay
for the pony. *Alfie* said to *Alice*, "Quick jump on the
back," which they did and had a great ride all the way
round the fair and could see everything. They saw the
merry-go-round, swings and a slide. All the children
were having so much fun. The trumpets blew again and
the mayor called to the children to go to the main arena
for the maypole dancing. *Alice* said, "I would love to
do that."

Suddenly they jumped off the trap and hid behind the straw bales again. As they looked into the arena they saw a large tall pole with dozens of silk ribbons hanging from it. As the children started running across to the maypole *Alice* jumped up and was dragged along with them. The children each grabbed one of the silk ribbons. *Alice* had the last one and nobody even noticed her as they danced round and round with the music playing. *Alfie* sat by a straw bale, laughing. *Alice* made sure that she ran back to *Alfie* before the children had finished.

There was one more stall left which was the wooden skittles. The children were throwing wooden balls to knock the skittles down. *Alfie* looked at *Alice* and said, "No, you are not, we have got to get back." They arrived back at Jacques's stall as he was just starting to clear away, so they jumped back into the bucket as he lifted it into the back of the van. *Alice* said to *Alfie,* "That is the best day we have ever had." When they arrived back at the windmill they were too tired to do anything else and they fell fast asleep.

The rag dolls were lying on the windowsill when they were awoken by a shining light. It was the moon and he said, "I was watching you both today, you are so lucky to have each other. Nichole sends her love from the star above and says, "Twinkle, twinkle little star, *Alice* and *Alfie*, I am watching you from afar."

Alice and *Alfie* A Day on the River

One warm spring morning *Alice* and *Alfie* got up early. Jacques had gone fishing with one of his friends, so they climbed down the ladder at the side of the window and ran round the back of the windmill. To their surprise all the daffodils and tulips were all flowering in amazing colours. *Alice* said to *Alfie*, "They are so beautiful."

Tied up at the side of the mill there was a little boat with rowing oars. *Alice* said, "Can we get into the boat, *Alfie* and pretend we are going down the river?" *Alfie* replied, "Yes, as long as you don't rock the boat."

Alfie got in first and the boat rocked from side to side. Then *Alice* stepped into the boat and as she sat down she knocked the rope off the hook which was moored to the wooden jetty. All of a sudden the boat started to move and they began to float down the river. *Alfie* said, "Ho, Ho, Ho, and off we go," but *Alice* looked scared and said to *Alfie,* "I'm frightened." They were taken by surprise when Mr. Otter jumped up and said, "Don't worry, I will look after you." He told them to grab the oars and row the boat.

The rag dolls watched fish jumping in and out of the water as Mr. Otter played with his friends the ducklings and swans.

The sky started to get darker and darker and then it began to rain. There was a loud bang and they saw amazing colours streak across the sky. There were blues, reds, pinks, greens and all different colours. *Alice* said to Mr. Otter, "What is that?"
He said, "It is called a rainbow and they say that at the end there is a pot of gold."

Alice and *Alfie* rowed over to the side of the riverbank, where they all got out and Mr. Otter asked "Can I come too?"

Alice said, "Of course," and as they walked along the riverbank it stopped raining. They could still see the rainbow and it was getting nearer and nearer. Suddenly the colours were shining onto *Alice* and *Alfie* and Mr. Otter said, "Stop, stop! You are at the end of the rainbow." As *Alice* turned there was a small pot of gold by her feet. She picked it up and the rainbow went flying up into the sky and disappeared. They carried the pot of gold back to the boat and carried on down the river.

In the distance they heard some bells ringing and up on a hill they saw a little church, so they stopped to listen to the bells ringing. As they got nearer the church they could hear children crying. *Alfie* opened the door and in the courtyard of the church there was a crowd of small boys and girls. The rag dolls hid behind the pillar, and saw a little lady and her friends dressed in white robes. Mr. Otter told the rag dolls they were the nuns who looked after the children.

That night lightning had hit the church roof and destroyed it. The nuns had told the children that they would have to live somewhere else and that was why they were crying. The children all shouted, "Why? Why?" and the nuns told them it was because they had no moncy to rcbuild thc roof.

Alice looked at *Alfie* and said, "Let them have the pot of gold and build the new roof." So Mr. Otter took the pot of gold over to the nuns and said it was a gift to them from *Alice* and *Alfie* children with big hearts who live at the magical windmill.
The nuns asked Mr. Otter if there was anything they could do for *Alice* and *Alfie*. He told them that they would like them to pray that one day they would be reunited with their friend Nichole. The nuns said they would pray for them and they would tell Nichole in their prayers.

As the rag dolls got back to the boat the bells of the church started ringing again. They could hear the children in the distance laughing and singing. Mr. Otter said, "What a lovely day," and he helped them all the way back to the windmill.

Alfie tied the boat up and they went upstairs to their bedroom. Jacques the windmill keeper was fast asleep and as they lay on the windowsill they fell fast asleep. The moon shone down again and tapped on the window, *Alice* woke up and opened the window. The moon said, "Nichole's star has told me that he has heard from the nuns and that you are both well and she sends her love."

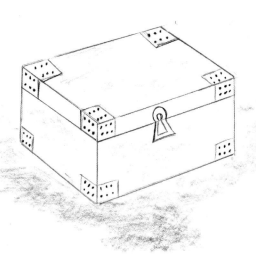

Alice and *Alfie* and the Magic Box

It had been a long day for *Alice* and *Alfie*. They
had played with the kittens and mice all around the
windmill. Jacques, the windmill keeper, had been to
an antique fair. They watched him unload the van and
decided that when he went to bed they would go and
look at what he had bought.

Soon, Jacques was fast asleep, so they went downstairs but there was nothing new on the table. They looked everywhere but it was just the same old things that were always there. *Alfie* said, "Perhaps he has put them in the barn." So they crept outside and opened the barn doors and there in the corner was a big metal chest. *Alfie* said, "Shall we open it?" *Alice* said, "Yes, let's." They lifted up the lid and there inside was an old lantern, two pictures and an old toy drum.

As they lifted out the antique pieces, right at the bottom was a beautiful wooden box glowing in lovely colours. They lifted it out and put it onto a bale of straw. *Alice* said, "Open it." So *Alfie* lifted the lid.

All of a sudden a glow of light shone at the entrance to the barn doors. They went to have a look and they saw it was the moon. He said he was passing by when he saw the colours of the box glowing. "I have seen that box before on my travels. It is a magical box and you must say the magic words, "Hocus pocus pudding and pie, take us on a journey so we can fly."

As they said these words, the little wooden box got bigger and bigger; the lid opened fully and inside the box was a glow of colour. The box had grown so big the moon said, "Quick, jump in."

All of a sudden there was a flash of light and two big ears and a trunk popped out of the box and screamed, "Boo, how are you?" It made *Alice* and *Alfie* jump and they fell to the floor.

When they stood up, *Alice* said, "Who are you?"
"My name is Elle the elephant and I live in the magic
box. Would you both like to look inside?" he said. As
they got in Elle shouted, "Quick! We must go," and the
lid fell down. *Alfie* asked why they had to go. "I
am being followed by a wicked witch." *Alice* looked
through the keyhole and there she saw in front of them
the wicked witch. She had a big black coat blowing in
the wind and a large black hat. *Alice* could not believe
it, she was flying on a broomstick and with a scream
and a wicked laugh she flew off into the distance.

Elle told the rag dolls that the witch was horrible. "Her name is OLIVE she gives out bad spells. "Anyway don't let's talk about horrible things. Here we go," and with a woosh and a wish they flew up into the sky. *Alice* said to *Alfie*, "Look through the keyhole. We are flying." They flew amongst the clouds and then dropped to the ground with a large bang. The lid opened and they all climbed out. Elle said, "We have landed at the mad professor's house, he makes up magical potions and nice spells but don't be frightened as he's a very nice man."

Elle and the rag dolls went up to the front door of the professor's house. There was a note on the door, "Please knock quietly. I am sleeping." *Alice* said to Elle, "That's strange, how will he hear us?" Elle knocked on the door with her trunk. After a while, the mad professor opened it. He looked out and said "Not today thank you," and shut the door. Elle opened the letterbox and shouted, "It's me Elle, the elephant." The door opened again and the professor told them never to forget the elephant. He said, "Come in," and sat them down in front a big log fire and asked them if they had eaten. They all said no and so he went off to cook them a lovely meal.

The professor put a big black pot onto the open fire. He poured in some water then, rats and mice and some things nice. *Alice* said *to Alfie*, "I will eat the nice but not the rats or mice!" As their dinner was cooking Elle talked about the witch called OLIVE. The mad professor said, "Don't worry about her. I'll sort her out," and he cast a magical spell. He said, "RATS AND BATS AND PENGUIN BEAKS LET OLIVE DISAPPEAR WITHOUT A SCREECH!"

He bottled up the spell and gave it to them and told them if she comes near you on the way home, "Just say the magic words and cover her with the potion." The mad professor said I am ready for bed. Elle said, "We must go now before it gets too dark," so *Alice* and *Alfie* said goodbye.

All three jumped into the box and flew off into the
sky through the clouds and all of a sudden there was
OLIVE, flying past and looking evil. Elle opened
the lid and as the witch flew over, *Alice* shouted the
magic words and *Alfie* threw the spell and the witch
disappeared with a loud pop.
They arrived back at the windmill and said goodbye
to Elle and with a flash of light the box went back to
its normal size. The moon shone down as they walked
back to the mill. He blew a kiss and said it was from
Nichole whom he knew they missed.

"*Alfie*, I think Elle the elephant is special."

Alice and *Alfie* Go to the Seaside

Alice was woken by a sound she had never heard before. The rag dolls looked out of the window and there by the river was a large bird with feathers and a red-feathered head. It was going 'cock-a-doodle-do', and was waking everybody up, even the fish in the river. *Alice* and *Alfie* heard Jacques go out of the door of the windmill and say to himself, "That noisy cockerel has come back again." By the time he had finished cock-a-doodle-doing everybody was awake.

Jacques had to make flour that day; he set in motion the wheels that started turning the big sails on the windmill. The noise was very loud. *Alice* said to *Alfie,* "I could not stand the noise of the cockerel and the windmill. Let's go out for the day."

Alice and *Alfie* climbed down the ladder at the side of the window and walked along the side of the riverbank. Two big birds flew down in front of them. *Alice* said to them, "What sort of birds are you?" as she had never seen birds like that before. They told her they were seagulls. *Alfie* said, "Where do you live?" and they told him that they lived by the seaside. *Alice* said, "What is the seaside?" One seagull told them that it is where there is a sandy beach and seawater and where children love to play with the sand and in the water.

Alice asked, "How do we get there?"

The birds replied that it was a very long way and it will take a long time to walk there. "If you like we could take you there," they said.

Alfie asked, "How can you take us?"

They replied, "Jump on our backs and we will fly you there." *Alice* said to *Alfie*, "Please, please can we?"

Alfie agreed to go and so they jumped up onto the back of the birds who said, "Up, up and off we go. Hold on tight and we will be there before you know."

The birds flew over the magic windmill and saw the sails going round. They showed the birds where they lived and the seagulls told them that they would bring them back safe. They flew over the magic castle and for one moment they thought they spotted the horrible witch OLIVE, but it was only a flash of the magician's spells that came from the castle.

As they flew, they saw the sea in the distance. It was shining blue and bright. The seagulls landed on the beach behind some rocks and told the rag dolls to be careful because the tide goes in and out. They said they would be back that night to pick them both up and off they flew up, up and away.

As *Alice* and *Alfie* looked over the top of the rocks they could see children playing and swimming in the sea. They had buckets and spades and flags.
Alice said to *Alfie,* "Can we go and play with the buckets and spades in the sand?" He agreed but he told her they must make sure the children did not see them.

The rag dolls built sand castles and put the flags on the top of them. All of a sudden they saw the children coming back, and they ran and hid behind some rocks. They heard them talking, "Who has made these beautiful sand castles?" They looked around but nobody was there. The children said to one another it must be magic. *Alice* started to giggle, and *Alfie* whispered to her to be quiet.

Alice felt something tickle her feet and she looked down and saw a large crab. The crab looked up at her and said, "Don't be scared of me, I won't bite as long as you don't eat me."

Alice replied, "Why would we want to eat you?"

"Mummies and daddies do. That is why I run sideways so they can't catch me."

Alice said, "Can you show us how you run sideways so they can't catch you?" The crab showed them his sideways run and they had never laughed so much. He said, "It does work, you know. I am over twenty years old and have never been on a plate yet.   Anyway I must go now as my dinner is coming in on the next tide."

All the children had gone and had left a small boat on the sand. The tide was coming in fast and it was pushing the boat nearer and nearer some rocks. All of a sudden *Alice* and *Alfie* realised that they were stranded. *Alice* said, "Quick, grab the boat" and they both jumped in. The tide was pushing them out to sea and they started to get frightened.

It was cold and getting dark and in the distance the sun was going down. *Alice* said, "I wish we were back at the windmill," and she began to cry.

There was a flash of light and the moon came down and said, "Don't be frightened, the seagulls are on their way." The rag dolls looked up in the sky and they spotted the seagulls flying towards them.
They landed on the boat, and one said, "Jump on our backs and we will take you to the windmill."

The rag dolls lay on the windowsill and *Alice* said,
"What a lovely day." *Alfie* agreed and said goodnight.
Suddenly the moon tapped on the window and said to
them, "Remember, the beach is fun but the sea is the
boss, so never make him cross."
"Go to sleep have sweet dreams. Nichole is near so do
not fear, God bless you."

"Oh, *Alice*, wasn't Mr. Crab funny?"

Alice and *Alfie* and the Magic Garden

Alice and *Alfie* were awoken by a horse and cart outside. The horse was going ney, ney, ney whilst it was eating its hay. The horse's name was Neddie and he belonged to the baker. The baker had arrived to collect the sacks of flour that Jacques had made the day before. The baker said to Jacques, " I have hurt my back. Would you be good enough to load the flour up and help me unload it too?" Jacques said he would and off they went.

Alice heard what they were saying and said to *Alfie,* "We have got the windmill to ourselves. What shall we do?"

Alfie answered, "Let's look around."

The rag dolls got to the bottom of the stairs and noticed a doorway they had never seen before, "It's because there was always a curtain across it," *Alice* said. *Alfie* tried to open the door but it was locked. *Alice* said, "Let's go and look for the key. It must be somewhere." They searched around the room but they couldn't find it anywhere.

Alice was upset but *Alfie* said, "Never mind." Just then, under the table, there was a squeak, squeak, squeak. It was the two little mice. The mice said, "It's a magic door, you do not need a key you just have to say the magic words."

Alice replied, "Please tell us!" The mice shouted together, "Door-a-door-a, unlock so we can explor-a." As the mice spoke the door slowly opened and the rag dolls walked into a secret garden.

There were butterflies flying everywhere. One flew into *Alice's* hand and said, "Please don't try to catch us. We are very delicate but you can run with us." As they ran along they saw rabbits having a field day in the vegetable patch, eating the carrots, lettuces and cabbage. *Alfie* asked them, "Does Jacques mind you eating all his vegetables?"

One rabbit replied, "No, this is a magic garden." And as he pulled up a carrot to eat, up popped another one! *Alfie* could not believe his eyes. *Alice* said, "This must indeed by a magic garden," and as they walked on they could smell the beautiful roses, daisies and buttercups in the field where the rabbits were running around.

At the end of the garden they heard a commotion.
They saw a large green grass area and a game of
some sort was going on. At one end there were three
stumps with a piece of wood on top of all three. At
the other end there was one piece of wood. Mr. Rabbit
was holding a wooden ball and at the other end Mr.
Hedgehog was holding a bat of some sort.
Alice and *Alfie* sat and watched Mr. Rabbit throw the
ball and Mr. Hedgehog hit it with the bat. *Alfie* asked
the other animals that were sitting close by how the
game was played. One time the ball nearly hit *Alfie*
on the head. *Alfie* shouted out, "How's that?" and all
the other animals thought he had caught the ball, but he
hadn't.

He laughed when he realised you had to catch the ball and when he had shouted, "How's that?" it meant he caught Mr. Rabbit out but of course he hadn't caught it. *Alice* said to *Alfie*, "I think we ought to leave before you mess the game up."

"Look over there, *Alfie*, at the cricket house. There is a table with lots of food and drink on it." They went over to have a look and found Mr. Tortoise sitting on a chair waiting to play the game. He said he was next to bat but after him it was lunch and they could all have something to eat. Mr. Tortoise said to *Alfie* and *Alice*, "You can stay and have some if you like?" *Alfie*, replied "Try and stop us."

Mr. Tortoise saw Mr. Hedgehog caught out and he walked slowly out onto the cricket pitch. Mr. Rabbit threw the ball and he was out for a duck. *Alice* said, "I didn't see the duck. Where is it?"

Mr. Hedgehog answered, "It is a saying when you are out for the very first time without scoring any runs." The rag dolls had a lovely tea with all the animals and then went on their way.

Alice and Alfie saw apple and plum trees in an orchard and they tried to pick some of the plums but could not reach. In a tall tree sat a black and white bird called Mr. Magpie and he had a word with Mr. Squirrel who then ran up the tree and dropped some plums down to Alice and Alfie. It was a magic tree and the plums grew back on the tree instantly. Alfie said to Alice, "It is getting late. We must be getting back to the windmill."

When they got back, they shut the garden door and started walking up the stairs. As they were half way Jacques walked onto the landing and the rag dolls fell to the floor and he nearly tripped over them. Jacques picked them up and took them back to the bedroom and said to himself, "The windmill's magic is still working, always moving things around."

Alice and *Alfie* fell asleep on the windowsill and that night the moon shone down along with Nichole's star and said, "Shining bright. When you wake up you will see the light, love Nichole."

"*Alice*, How's that for a game of cricket?"

Alice and *Alfie*
When you Wish upon a Star

It had been nearly a year since Nichole had gone back home and said she would be back but *Alice* and *Alfie* knew in their hearts they might never see her again. Then one morning they heard Jacques on the telephone, he was talking to Nichole's mummy and daddy. He said he would love them to come and visit. *Alice* heard the conversation and she told *Alfie.* They could not believe Nichole was coming back to stay and they both jumped for joy. *Alice* said, "Hip, hip, hooray. Nichole's coming to stay."

The day arrived and Nichole was coming back to them. *Alice* and *Alfie* could not believe it; it had been such a long time.   Then the telephone rang and Jacques answered it. He said, "Never mind, another time," It appeared that Nichole's daddy was not well and the family had had to cancel their trip.

All afternoon *Alice* cried and cried and cried. *Alfie* did not know what to do. That evening they sat at the window staring out and thinking of all the exciting things they had done. The mice came and sat with them; the seagulls landed on the windowsill too but still *Alice* kept crying. Then it grew dark and the moon came down and asked *Alice*, "What is the matter?" She told him that Nichole could not come after all. The moon said, "Don't be sad *Alice*, why not draw some happy faces,"

"How do you mean?" said *Alfie.*

The moon said, "Get a round glass and draw a circle around it. Now draw some hair and then a face on it." *Alice* drew a headband on hers and *Alfie* put a hat on his. "They look just like yourselves now," said the moon, "You are laughing and happy. Now I want you to close your eyes and pretend these faces are you," and so they did. "Now open your eyes." he said. They found they were both floating with the moon in the sky and they could not believe it. The moon flew and flew and they went up into the sky and reached the magic star shining bright.

The moon called to them, "Nichole's star is shining bright, make your wish tonight." They made their wish and the moon told them that when you wish upon a star your wish comes true, wherever you are. The moon knew what they had wished for and he blew and he blew until they were fast asleep.

When *Alice* and *Alfie* woke up they were in Nichole's bedroom. They fell to the floor and there they lay forever asleep with dreams of the magic windmill. The moon had made their wish come true.

Alice and *Alfie* Holiday Time again

Alice and *Alfie* had been back at Nichole's house for about six months when the summer arrived. *Alice* heard Nichole say to her mummy, "Can we go back to France and stay at the windmill for our holiday this year?" Then just as her mummy answered, the door slammed in the wind and *Alice* could not hear anymore.

Alice shouted to *Alfie* , "Nichole is going back to
France to the magical windmill."
Alfie said, "I cannot wait."
That evening Nichole's mummy talked to her daddy
about the holiday, and he said he had already booked a
special holiday somewhere else. Nichole was so upset
she went upstairs to her bedroom and she lay on her bed
and cried.

Later Nichole got up and went over to *Alice* and *Alfie* and said, "No France this year, we are going to a special place that daddy has booked," but *Alice* and *Alfie* were fast asleep and did not hear a thing. The holiday arrived and all their cases were packed. *Alice* said, "Quick, *Alfie*, lie down. I think we are off to France." They lay in their box in the corner of the room and waited and waited and waited. Later they heard the front door shut and *Alice* said, "Oh no, no, no. They have left us behind again! I don't believe it!" That night, *Alice* just cried and cried. *Alfie* said "Go to sleep and everything will seem better in the morning."

There was a tap, tap, tap, on the window. It was their friend the moon so they opened the window and the moon asked, "*Alice*, what is the matter, why are you crying?" *Alfie* told him what had happened and that Nichole and her mummy and daddy had gone back to France for their holiday. *Alice* said, "We wanted to go back too." The Moon said "Let's do the magic moon spell." So they all said together, "When you wish upon a star your dream would come true, so take us far."

The moon blew and blew and to the windmill they flew. The rag dolls landed back in the windmill, thanked the moon and sat on the windowsill and quickly fell asleep.

The next morning they woke up and opened the bedroom door, but heard nothing. They went downstairs and found there was nobody there. There was no Nichole, no mummy and daddy and no Jacques the windmill keeper. His van had also gone. They ran round the windmill to the front door. There was a note on the door and it said, 'Gone away for three weeks, don't knock or you will wake the cats.'

Alice and *Alfie* went round the windmill to the back door and into the kitchen. The kittens had grown into cats, and they were fast asleep on their mats. *Alice* woke them up. She said, "Do you remember us?" and the cats said yes they did. *Alice* said, "If Jacques is away, who is feeding you?"

The cats replied, "Don't worry, we have been eating the mice and they taste very nice."

Alice said, "No, no, no," and the cats laughed and laughed and said they were only joking. They were being fed by the lady down the road. The cats asked them why they had come back and *Alice* told them the story.

That night as it grew dark *Alice* and *Alfie* went to
sleep. They dreamt of all the things they had done
and the adventures they had had. When they woke up
Alice said, "The wooden prince, let's go back and see
him." So they went downstairs and got some apples
and water and off they went.

The rag dolls walked over the old bridge and along
the beach and at last, there it was in the distance: the
magic castle. The rag dolls still had the problem of
getting across the water; so they lay on the grassy bank
of the river and stared into the water. All of a sudden
the water started to ripple and from nowhere stepping
stones appeared. They ran across them to the castle
gate, where they knocked on the door and it opened
before them.

In front of the rag dolls stood a tall man in a long black coat and a large pointed hat. He said, "Yes, can I help you would you like a spell?" *Alice* told him she could already spell and he laughed and said, "No, not spelling words; I can cast spells which will give you good luck and things you would like."

Alice said, "We would like to see the wooden prince."
He said "Come in, he is sleeping in the fireplace."
Alfie was surprised, "Why? what if somebody lights the fire?"

"No, no, no" he answered, "He lies in there because he still thinks he is a log of wood."

Alice said, to him, "What is your name?"
He told them, "My name is Professor Wood Eye."
Alfie laughed, "Have you got a wooden eye?"

He said, "No, but when I was young my mother gave me the name because of the time she asked me, "would I do this and would I do that."

At that moment the wooden prince woke up and sat up in the fire place. *Alice* said to him, "How are you?"
He said, "I feel great after my sleep." He stared at the rag dolls and said, "Hello, I remember you. You must stay for dinner."

144

Alice and Alfie sat at the table eating and talking. After a while the professor said he was going to his room down in the cellar to the castle to make up some spells. Alice said, "Can we come too?" So they all went down a small stone staircase into the cellar.

It was cold and damp and dark. Alfie said, "I'm freezing." and Alice said she was too. Professor Wood Eye shouted out, "Boom, boom, warm the room." There was a flash of light and some smoke and the room became warm and light.
Alice was amazed, "Wow! That's magic." she said. Professor Wood Eye started mixing his spells. The wooden prince was upstairs he could not come down as normally it would be too cold and damp for him and all his joints would rot.

A few minutes later the professor waved his wand and there was a loud bang. He poured the potion he was mixing into a large bottle. He filled it right to the top, and then said, "Oh, no!" *Alice* asked him what was wrong and he replied, "I've made too much.
The potion will have to be used."

The professor said there would be at least three wishes in the bottle. He then asked whether they would like three wishes. And the rag dolls cried, "Yes, please." Professor Wood Eye said, "Are you ready then make your three wishes one, two, three, give your wishes to me."

1. *Let everybody love each other.*

2. *Give the wooden prince a special coating so he can go out in the cold and wet.*

3. *To go on a magical trip with the wooden Prince.*

The professor waved his magic wand and made their dreams come true and the wooden prince was free to go to sea.

That night they went to bed early and they fell fast asleep.

The moon tapped on the window but *Alice* and *Alfie* didn't hear that he had said, "Sleep tight tonight for tomorrow will be bright and your dreams will come true and Nichole is thinking of you."

Alice and *Alfie*

The Wooden Prince's Dream

Alice and *Alfie* were fast asleep when they were awoken by a bright light at the window. It was the mad professor from the magic castle. He waved his magic wand and cried, "Make three wishes and I will make your wishes come true."

In no time they found themselves on an old ship far out to sea. They hid in a corner by the kitchen door. Inside the kitchen a chef was cooking fish that made a horrible whiff. The chef saw them hiding in the corner and took them to the captain. The captain said, "Hang them up till they tell us who they are."

Alice cried, "Oh, please don't hurt us"

And *Alfie* asked, "Why are you so horrible?"

The captain replied, "We are horrible because we are pirates of the sea, and we can't be nice" and with that all the pirates laughed and laughed.

The captain said, "I will ask you again, where do you come from?" *Alfie* told him, "From the magic windmill up on the hill."
The captain laughed, "Magic windmill? Pigs might fly!" He told his pirates to leave them hanging there till morning.

Alice and *Alfie* cried and cried. They heard the captain and his men drinking and laughing down in their cabins. Just then out in the darkness they heard "pst. pst. pst." At first they thought it was the cats, but then they saw it was the wooden prince. *Alice* said quietly, "What are you doing out here in the cold and wet. You will just rot and fall to pieces."

The wooden prince replied, "No, I won't. I woke up this morning with a special coat of varnish all over my body, so now I can go outside."

There was a storm brewing out in the distance and the ship rocked from side to side. The wooden prince had been reunited with the rag dolls. He released them and went down with them into the hull of the ship. In the corner was the captain's bounty. There was a large coconut, gold and silver coins and also rings and chains shining bright. They all lay on the old sheet in the corner and fell asleep.

The next morning the captain and his men went on deck and one of the men shouted, "Look the prisoners have gone." The ropes were swaying in the wind and the captain said they must have fallen overboard in the storm last night.

Alice heard the men saying that they were going to throw the captain off the ship tonight. *Alfie* said to her, "That is not very nice."

As night fell the captain stood on the bridge with his
hands wrapped around the big wheel that steered the
ship. All of a sudden the pirates started to fight. The
captain and his mate stood their ground and they turned
the cannon and fired it at the pirates. The cannonball
went straight up into the air and it just missed *Alice*
and *Alfie*. The cannonball flew past the wooden
prince and shot through the bottom of the ship.

There was a loud crash and the rag dolls could see that it had made a large hole and that seawater was coming in. The ship was sinking and the captain said to all the pirates, "Abandon ship."

They all shouted, "Aye, Aye captain."

Alice and *Alfie* called to the prince, "Look there is a plank of wood hanging over the side of the ship." They all ran onto it. The captain saw them and he ran over with a hammer and hit the wooden plank. It snapped in two and fell into the sea. The rag dolls and the wooden prince all hung onto it and as it floated away they could see the ship in the distance, slowly sinking into the sea and heard the captain shouting "Please save me!"

All night they clung onto the plank of wood and eventually fell asleep.

They were awoken by the sound of birds calling and they found themselves lying on a beach. The brightly coloured birds were called parrots.

The prince stood up and said, "I feel as if I have been here before you know." He went to sit under a tree out of the hot sun, *Alice* and *Alfie* followed. As they lay there, they heard a loud noise from above. *Alice* and *Alfie* looked up and there in the tree was a grumpy old monkey called Love.

The monkey grabbed a coconut shell and dropped it from above and it landed right on *Alfie's* head. *Alfie* cried, "That hurt, you little monkey." The monkey climbed down and said he was sorry but he only wanted them to have something to eat and drink. *Alice* said, "What is in the coconut?"

Alfie said, "It must be a brick because my head still hurts." The monkey showed them how to open the coconut and they sat and enjoyed the milk and fruit.

Alice and *Alfie* sat and told the monkey where they came from and *Alice* asked the monkey where he lived. He said, "I live in the trees with the bees and all my friends, would you like to meet them?" They all said they would so they walked through the woods looking up into all the trees. The parrots sang beautifully as they went on their way.

Eventually they came to a clearing in the woods where there were mud huts with straw roofs. The monkey told them that this was where the witch doctor lived. *Alice* said, "Which doctor?" and the monkey just laughed. The monkey told them that he was kind and he might let them stay. He knocked on the door and the witch doctor shouted out, "Who is there?"

The monkey answered, "Open the door and you will see."

The witch doctor said, "See who"

And the monkey replied, "You will see us" and with that he opened the door and let them in where they all sat and talked. He said they could stay with him and he would love to hear about their adventures.

The monkey told the two rag dolls, "I must go now but I will come back later with my friends."

The wooden prince had been looking around the woods. He knocked on the door of the wooden hut and the witch doctor opened the door and shouted, "The Prince, the Prince, the Prince," and he bowed his head. *Alice* said, "Do you know him?"

And the witch doctor replied ,"Yes, he is the Prince of the Island." He told them that he was taken away twenty years ago by the pirates. The Prince said "I can't remember anything about that but when we arrived here I thought I had been here before."

That night the witch doctor played his drums, which called to all the animals on the island to come to a party to celebrate the return of the prince.

The monkeys were first to arrive they were playing their drums and trumpets. The parrots came flying in and the eagles too, followed by three bears. They hugged the prince and shouted, "The Prince, the Prince." They sang and danced all night and told stories. The prince was so happy because now he was varnished he could live there forever without rotting and falling apart.

The witch doctor and all his friends built *Alice* and *Alfie* a boat so they could sail back to the magical windmill. They got into the boat and said goodbye to everyone. The prince was crying although he was very happy. *Alice* and *Alfie* said they would be back one day as they sailed off into the sunset.

As they sailed across the sea they saw a large piece of wood floating in the distance. As they got nearer they heard someone singing, "I'm a pirate of the sea, give your gold and silver to me."

Alice said, "It is that pirate that hung us up on the ship." The pirate pleaded with them to give him a helping hand and *Alice* and *Alfie* helped him into the boat. They tied his hands once he got on board the boat so he could be put in prison for robbery and treason. They dropped him off in a port and off they went on their way.

On the way back up the river they went past the castle where the wooden prince once lived and soon they were home at the magic windmill. They lay in the window and were nearly off to sleep when the moon floated down and they told him of their adventures. He said, "Sleep well, sleep tight because Nichole's star is shining bright."

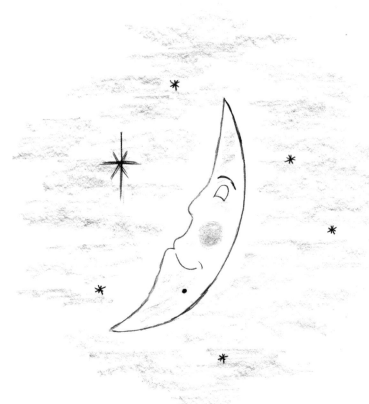

Alice and *Alfie*
The Circus Comes to Town

Alice and *Alfie* were awoken by the sound of the windmill grinding the corn to make flour for the baker to make bread and cakes. Jacques was working hard as he always did. *Alice* got up and went downstairs and she saw on the kitchen table a newspaper and on the front page it said in large letters THE CIRCUS IS IN TOWN – FREE TICKETS INSIDE. The paper said animals, clowns and merry-go-rounds and monkeys too.

Alice ran upstairs to tell *Alfie* but he was fast asleep. *Alice* shook him and shouted, "Pst, pst, pst." and he woke and said, "That is not my name!"

She told him that the circus had come to town, so they both went downstairs to have another look at the paper. They read about the free tickets on page four. As they turned the pages they saw that someone had cut out the free tickets, "Oh, no" said *Alice*, "Now we can't go to the circus. They looked around but could not see them.

The kitchen door opened. It was Jacques, so they fell
to the floor and Jacques tripped over them. He picked
them up and put them on the magic carpet in front of
the fire. He muttered to himself, "The windmill has
been up to its tricks again." He looked at *Alice* and
Alfie, "Do you know I have lost three pairs of glasses
and my van keys twice. They must be somewhere in the
windmill." He then had a cup of tea and a cake and
went back to the mill to make some flour.

After Jacques had gone, *Alice* heard a squeak, squeak, squeak and lots of giggling. *Alfie* said,

"Good morning, why are you laughing so much?"
The mice told him to wait a minute and ran back into their hole in the wall and come running back into the kitchen wearing Jacques's glasses. *Alice* could not stop laughing and asked, "Have you got his keys too?"
They said they had and *Alice* said, "You must give them back.

Alfie said, "You should because you cannot drive."
The mice replied, "We can now because we have got glasses." But they decided to give them back and left them on the table.

Alice said to the mice, "The circus has come to town, but we have no tickets," and they showed the mice the paper. The mice said all they had to do was go early. "Do you remember your friend Elle the elephant. Look, she is in the show. She will let you in free." All of a sudden the cats ran through the back door. The mice said, "Run, run, run so the cats don't have their fun," and they ran into the hole in the wall. The cats waited and waited by the hole until they fell asleep.

The next day was the first day of the circus. *Alice* and *Alfie* set off early down the ladder, along the riverbank, towards the town. They met Mr. Hedgehog chasing a frog. They told him where they were going and he said he would love to come too. Then they met Mr. Squirrel, who was sat on the wall playing the fiddle. Mr. Otter also heard what they said and he started walking with them.

The rag dolls and their friends all arrived at the village green and there was a big tent with flags flying and a sign saying, "Welcome to the big circus." There was a very long queue with mummies and daddies and children too. Everyone had a ticket except *Alice* and *Alfie.*

When they arrived at the village green they looked for Elle the elephant but could not see her. Then all of a sudden they heard the trumpet blowing. It was Elle and she was inside the tent.

Alice said, "We are never going to get in there now," and she started to cry.

Alfie told her, "Don't cry, *Alice.* "

and she sobbed, "But we won't be able to see the show without tickets." They all sat down and started to think of how to get into the circus when all of a sudden the ground started rumbling and there was dirt and soil flying everywhere. They heard a squeak, squeak, squeak, they all thought it was the mice but they were at home.

After the soil had stopped flying about Mr. And Mrs. Mole popped their heads out. *Alice* told them what had happened. Mr. Mole said, "No problem, we will get you in there."

Alice asked, "How?"

Mr. Mole said to Mrs. Mole, "dig, dig, dig," and they all followed. They all squeezed through the tunnel and up into the tent. The rag dolls and all the animals popped their heads up and they were right in the middle of the circus with the ringmaster, who looked very grand in his red jacket and big top hat.

They could see the whole show from here. First it was the bears, they sang a song but all of a sudden they stopped; they had forgotten their lines. So the ringmaster asked, "What's with the big pause?" and waving their paws about they replied, "because we are bears!"

Later, after the circus they walked back along the riverbank with the moon shining bright. They went up the ladder and soon went off to sleep. Later that night the moon shone down and went tap, tap, tap on the window. The moon said to *Alice*, "I see you went to the circus and met your friend Elle the elephant. You and *Alfie* looked as though you were having so much fun. Nichole is also laughing tonight with delight with her star shining bright."

"*Alfie*, stop clowning around."

Alice and *Alfie* Fireworks in the Sky

One night when it was very late and the sky was getting darker and darker, *Alice* and *Alfie* fell asleep on the windowsill. They were awoken by a loud bang, and a woosh and another bang. They looked out of the window but they could only see the stars. *Alfie* said, "What was that?" The moon saw them looking and he floated down to them. He said it was the loudest bang he had ever heard and told the rag dolls that it was a firework called a rocket. He said the next day would be November 5th, firework night, and that they were going to have a big party on the village green tomorrow night. *Alice* and *Alfie* told him that they would love to go and the moon said he would see them there and look out for them.

The next morning *Alice* and *Alfie* got up and decided to walk to the village to see what was going on. As they walked along the path through the woods, they heard an unusual sound. It was going cuckoo, cuckoo, cuckoo and coming from up in the trees. They saw a big bird and it flew down and sat with them on a wooden log and it went cuckoo, cuckoo again.

Alice said, "What is it with this cuckoo, cuckoo?"

"It is my name," the bird replied." *Alice* told him, "it is firework night tonight." The cuckoo got very upset at the thought of all those bangs and started shaking.

Alfie said, "Are you alright?"

"I hate fireworks because they wake me up and sometimes they follow me flying through the sky." He replied.

Alice said, "That must be fun," and with that the cuckoo flew off to tell his friends about the fireworks so they could hide in the trees.

Alice and *Alfie* carried on walking until they reached
the village green. There they saw many tents, some
with food, some with drinks and right at the end of the
green was an area that had been roped off with a sign
saying, 'Beware Fireworks.' They decided to walk
to the edge of the woods and wait till it was evening
where they both fell fast asleep under a tree.

Before long it got dark and they were awoken by the sound of hundreds of children with their mummies and daddies. They heard music playing and everyone was eating and drinking. All of a sudden there were catherine wheels spinning around to the music and all the children were going, "aww! Ahh! Wow!"

 There were coloured beams of light flashing up in the sky from the rockets. *Alice* said to *Alfie,* "Isn't it lovely?" as the fireworks got higher and higher.
Alfie said, "Look, there is the moon."
Alice shouted out, "Moon, moon get out of the way, or a rocket will take you to the Milky Way."

Alice and Alfie moved forward just as the man who was organising the display lit the last biggest firework to end the show. All of a sudden from nowhere Mr. Cuckoo flew down and tried to put it out.
Alice and Alfie ran to help and they jumped onto Mr. Cuckoo's back and steered him away from the rocket which was making a loud woosh, woosh, woosh.

As they were flying high they saw all the children below, watching the rocket let off all its colours. *Alice* loved it, but *Alfie* said, "The problem is, what goes up must come down." The rocket went flying past the moon, who was laughing. The moon followed them up into the sky and as the rocket started to slow the moon dropped down and said to *Alice* and *Alfie,* "Jump on my back and I will take you back." *Alfie* said, "That was lucky *Alice.*" And as they travelled back to the windmill the moon told them all about the stars and planets.

The moon told them about the Milky Way and said it was too far away. He told them about the planet Mars and all the other stars, then out of the blue in front of them was an amazing shining star. The moon asked them, "You know whose star that is?"

Alice said, "It's Nichole's star"

"Yes it was, you must make a wish as we go past."
The rag dolls closed their eyes and sang together "With a woosh and a wish, please give Nichole a kiss."
The moon lowered them gently onto the village green. The fireworks had finished and the party was over. All the children were walking home they were all saying how lovely the big rocket was.

186

Alice and *Alfie* set off again back to the windmill. Before they went off to sleep the moon said, "Goodnight and God bless and remember, remember the 5th November and remember fireworks are fun but only mummies and daddies must light one. Nichole sends her love woosh, woosh."

"*Alfie*, that rocket went off with a bang!"

Alice and *Alfie* and the Easter Egg Hunt

Alice and Alfie were playing in the windmill and Jacques had gone to market to sell bags of flour. They ran down the stairs and out to the back of the windmill. Alice said to Alfie, "Please start the sails so I can watch them go round on the windmill." Alfie went into the mill and turned the big wheel, and called to her, "Alice I have done it."

She shouted back, "Nothing is happening," so he went back inside and tried again. The wheel started to move but then stopped. Alice said to Alfie, "Help me push the sail at the bottom." It still didn't move at first so they both jumped onto it. All of a sudden the sails started to move, but it was too late for them to get off.

The wind blew and blew and blew as the hands turned faster and faster. *Alfie* called to the wind, "Can you make it stop please, as I am shaking at my knees." The wind said it would have to stop on its own, and round and round went the hands, faster and faster. *Alice* shouted, "I can't hang on any longer," and *Alfie* said, "I'm scared. I think we are going to crash to the floor."

The rag dolls could not hold on any longer and they
flew off the hands of the windmill and came down with
a crash and a bang and landed right on Mr. and Mrs.
Rabbit who were sitting in the magical garden. Mr.
Rabbit said, "You should watch where you are going
when you are flying."
Alice answered, "We are sorry, it was the wind's fault.
He blew and blew and blew."
Mr. Rabbit said, "Pigs might fly but not rag dolls."

There was a lot going on in the magical garden and *Alice* said, "Why is it so busy?"

Mrs. Rabbit replied, "It is the Easter egg hunt tomorrow and everybody has got to hide an egg. Afterwards all the children have to try and find them and the one who finds the most will win a prize. Would you like to hide some?" asked Mrs. Rabbit.

Alice and *Alfie* replied, "Oh yes please."

The rabbits gave them two chocolate eggs each to hide.
Alfie put his first egg in a hole in an apple tree and
two bees came flying out and stung him on the knees.
To hide his second egg he pulled up a carrot but by the
time he had put the egg down into the ground another
carrot had popped up. *Alfie* had forgotten it was a
magical garden, so he turned and put his second egg in
a bucket next to the shed.

Alice decided to put her two eggs in the hen house so the chickens would lay on them with their other eggs. The rag dolls told Mr. and Mrs. Rabbit that they would come back the next day to watch the children play.

The next day *Alice* and *Alfie* got up early. They crept down the stairs, opened the curtain at the bottom of the stairs and went through the door into the magical garden after saying the magic words.

The animals had already arrived and they all had their babies all in a line. There were ducklings, bunnies, chicks, piglets, baby hedgehogs and little baby squirrels.

All of a sudden Mr. Owl sitting on his perch shouted out, "Let the Easter egg hunt begin."
All the little animals started running everywhere, looking for the eggs. Mr. Cuckoo come flying in low and knocked Mr. Owl off his perch. *Alice* could not believe her eyes, the chickens were running around with chocolate on their bottoms. They had been sitting on the eggs and the chocolate ones had melted!

The wood lice had eaten the egg that *Alfie* had put in the apple tree and all that was left was the wrapper. The worms had eaten the egg under the bucket so they were two eggs down and that meant that some of the children would not get an egg. *Alice* said, "I will go back and find some more, *Alfie*." and off she went back to the windmill.

The sails had stopped going round on the windmill.
Alice crept into the kitchen. She looked on the kitchen
table and there were six chocolate Easter eggs. Jacques
had bought them for himself. They were only very
small so *Alice* quickly took two of them and put them
in her pocket. She rushed back into the secret garden
and hid them. It was the perfect end to the
Easter egg hunt as all the children found an egg each.
Alice said, "It is very EGGSCITING watching the
children playing games."

Later *Alice* and *Alfie* watched the egg and spoon race, roll the hedgehog to pop the balloons and the tug of war. It was the ducks against the piglets, and the sound was amazing. They were going quack, quack and honk, honk when all of a sudden the ducks pulled the piglets over the line to win.

The day was EGGSTRAORDINARY and everybody had a lot of fun. The pigs went home with a honk, honk, honk, the ducks said quack, quack, quack and the chickens scratched all the way home. Mr. Cuckoo just went cuckoo!

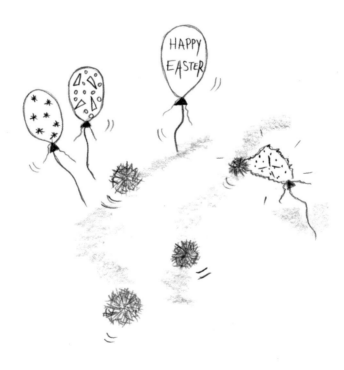

Alice and *Alfie* collected some vegetables for Jacques to replace the two Easter eggs that *Alice* had taken. They went back to the windmill and put the vegetables on the table next to the other Easter eggs. Suddenly they heard Jacques coming down the stairs and they fell to the floor and heard him say, "How can there be only four Easter eggs instead of six but vegetables in their place?"

Jacques said thank you to the magical windmill for the vegetables. He looked at the rag dolls and thought "That is funny; they have chocolate on their faces?" So he washed their faces and put them to bed on the windowsill.

Before *Alice* and *Alfie* fell asleep the moon shone down and said, "I saw what happened today and what fun you had at the Easter egg hunt. Nichole sends her love and two Easter eggs from above."

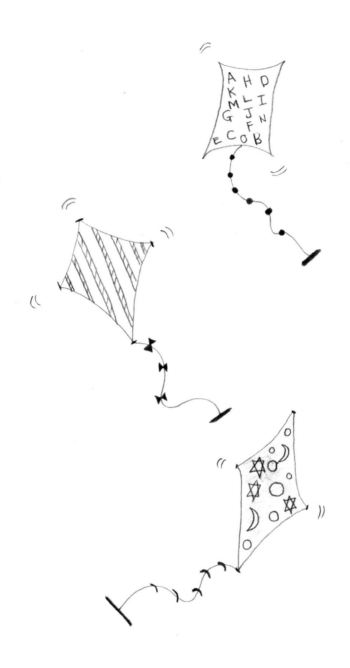

Alice and *Alfie* A day with the Kites

Alice and *Alfie* were awoken by the window shutters blowing in the wind. *Alice* said, "It is very windy outside *Alfie.*" As they looked out of the window to their amazement the leaves were falling off the trees. *Alice* said, "It is very sad, the trees loosing their leaves." They decided to wait until Jacques the windmill keeper started work and then they climbed down the ladder. The sails of the windmill were turning faster and faster.

The rag dolls heard Jacques talking in the mill. He was on the telephone and saying he could not make any flour because it was too windy and the windmill sails were going around too fast. He said, "but it is a good day for flying kites." *Alice* looked at *Alfie* and said "I wonder what he means by flying kites?"

Jacques said he would meet his friend and they would go fishing for the day instead.

All of a sudden the two cats came running round the corner and knocked *Alice* and *Alfie* over. The cats rolled and rolled and rolled down the riverbank and landed in the river. They got out, shook themselves off and *Alice* said to them, "What have you been up to?" The cats replied, "We have been chasing the mice." *Alice* cried, "Where are they, you haven't eaten them, have you?"

The cats smiled and said, "No, we have been playing cat and mouse in the house." The mice went squeak, squeak and shouted, "We are too quick for you."

Alice asked the cats, "Do you know what a kite is?"
The cats answered, "Yes, it is a piece of cloth with a
string on it. It has a handle and it flies in the sky."
Alfie said, "We have never seen them in the sky
before. Are they magic?"
The cats replied, "No, the children in the park play with
them."
"Then that is where we will go." said *Alice.*
The cats asked, "Can we come too?" And so off they
went to the park and with a squeak, squeak, squeak the
mice went too.

The rag dolls and their friends followed the pathway through the woods to the park. They heard children playing on the slide and the swings and the seesaw. Up on the hill there were other children and they were playing with their kites. They all sat down on the bench watching the kites fly. *Alice* said, "They are so magic, you know. Look at the way they go up and down and from side to side."

The cats answered, "Talking about side to side, shall we go on the seesaw now the children have gone?"

Alfie said, "Yes let's." But the sign on the gate said 'NO PETS!'

Within a moment the cats jumped on the seesaw and up and down they went. *Alice* jumped onto the swing and *Alfie* ran up the steps to the slide and when he got to the top he shouted, "Here I go, where I stop, I do not know." He slid down the slide and ended up on his bottom. After a while *Alice* said, "Where are the mice?" The cats looked around but said they could not see them. *Alfie* was worried and cried, "I can't hear them squeaking." So the cats set off to find them.

Some children were playing with their kites and then later their mummies and daddies came to take them home. *Alice* said, "Let's go up on the hill when they have gone?" *Alfie* followed *Alice*. The wind was blowing very hard. By the time they got to the top of the hill they could hardly stand up.

Over in the woods they could hear a little girl crying, so they went over to see what the matter was. The rag dolls hid behind a tree, her kite had blown away and landed in a tree. Her daddy told her that he would buy her a new one as it was too far up the tree for him to reach.

After the little girl and her daddy had gone *Alfie* said to *Alice*, "I wish we could get the kite down." *Alice* said, "I cannot reach it the kite is too far up." Suddenly out of the bushes ran the mice followed by the cats. *Alice* said, "Stop, stop look, there is a kite up in the tree. Please get it down for me?" The cats ran up the tree and in no time the kite was floating down to the ground.

Alice and Alfie walked with the animals up to the top of the hill. They laid the kite out on the grass and Alfie ran with it. It went up, up and away. The cats said," Fly, fly, fly like a butterfly." All of a sudden the wind dropped and the kite fell to the ground and Alice started to cry. The moon was high above and saw what happened. He shouted to the wind, "Alice and Alfie's kite is no longer in flight, so blow and blow with all your might."

The wind blew and blew but *Alfie* was not watching the kite and it started to move. *Alice* shouted, "Quick, catch the kite," but the cats missed it. *Alfie* jumped but also missed it and as it passed him by, the mice jumped on the handle and it went up high. The mice were flying in the sky. It was so funny!

Alice and *Alfie* and the two cats stood and scratched their heads. *Alice* said, "How are we going to get them down?"

"It looks like they will have to stay up there all night," replied the cats.

The mice were squeaking and squeaking. *Alice* shouted up to the moon, "Please help us. The mice are on the kite, and they could be up there all night." The moon shouted to the wind, "Will you stop blowing, please?"

The wind shouted back "Make your mind up. Do you want them to go up or down?"

"Let them down" the moon replied. The wind began to drop and the kite started to fall and with a big bang they came down to the ground.

The mice thanked the wind and they packed the kite up and *Alice* said, "We can come another day."
They all walked back to the magical windmill and they were all so tired they fell straight to sleep. Later that night the moon tapped on the window and said to *Alice* and *Alfie*, "Kites are nice, but not for mice.
Nichole sends her love from her shining star above."

"*Alice*, I can't wait for another windy day."

Alice and *Alfie* A Mess in the Kitchen

217

It was a lovely sunny morning and the birds were singing and for once the dreaded cock bird had gone away, so the alarm clock didn't go off. The windmill sails began to move. *Alice* said to *Alfie*, "Look, the windmill has started to work." and the wind blew and blew.

Jacques was in the mill making some flour. He had a friend with him called Kimmy, the lady from down the road. She was going to be making cakes all day. *Alice* heard her say to Jacques that there was a cake competition tomorrow on the village green and the winner will receive a big silver cup and some chocolates.

Alice and *Alfie* lay at the top of the stairs listening to them. Jacques said he was not going to bake but he would go and help her at her cottage. Off they went, flour bags and all.

Alice and *Alfie* crept downstairs and there in the corner were the mice eating cheese. *Alice* said, "You have both got dirty knees, so go and wash them please." *Alfie* cried, "Shall we try to bake a cake to take to the village green?"

Alice replied, "Yes, yes please but how do we make a cake *Alfie*?" The cats came running in and said it is as easy as one, two, three. *Alice* asked the cats to show her how it was done. They looked in the cupboards for the ingredients and everything was there apart from the flour. They went into the mill but there was none there. *Alfie* said, "I have watched Jacques grind the flour. Let us do it."

Alfie started the wheels and *Alice* went outside and asked the wind to blow, blow, blow, and he did. They put the grain onto the big stones and it started to grind and grind until they had the flour. *Alice* ran back outside and told the wind to stop blowing, he said, "Thank goodness for that, I was out of breath."

$Alice$ went back into the kitchen and the cats were playing on the magic carpet. They were rolling over and over and playing with the mice. That was so nice. $Alice$ put the flour in a big bowl when the door opened and in walked Mr. Mole. He had heard they were making cakes and decided to help. He had also brought along a very good mate, Mr. Snake.

The water went into the bowl, the butter too, and then the currents and cream and they mixed and mixed and mixed. All of a sudden Mr. Mole fell into the bowl and the flour went up into the air and covered the mice and the cats too. They all ran round the kitchen singing, "We're making cakes, so please let's be mates and clean the plates."

The cakes went in the oven till they were done and out they came one by one. They looked so good the cats said, "I think we should"
Alice shouted, "No, no, no we're taking them to the show, to win the cup and the chocolates too." *Alfie* took the cakes upstairs to the bedroom and hid them in the cupboard. The kitchen looked a mess.

Alice and *Alfie* asked the cats to leave, but the mice stayed and helped clean up and with a squeak, squeak, and they soon had the place looking like home, but before they could dry up the pots and pans and wash their feet and hands the door opened and there was Jacques.

 The rag dolls fell to the floor fast asleep. Jacques called out, "What has been going on? Pots and pans and dirty hands, I can't remember making this mess. It must be the windmill's magic."

"Never mind, I am going to bed. I have worked hard today making bread and cakes with Kimmy and friends."

Alice and *Alfie* were left on the floor but after
Jacques had gone they jumped up and went to bed.

The next morning they put their cakes into a bag and
climbed down the ladder at the side of the window.
They ran across to the barn and put the cakes in the
bucket in the back of Jacques' van. Jacques came
out and started the van. He was whistling and singing,
"Kimmy's going to win the cup and the chocolates too."
Alice whispered to *Alfie*, "Oh no she's not."

Jacques drove to the village green and there was a big
white tent with a sign saying CAKE COMPETITION.

Alice and *Alfie* ran round to the back of the tent. They lifted up the side sheet and went inside. There were so many tables. There were tables with bread, cakes, jams and pickles and there in the corner they saw Kimmy putting her cakes on a table. She had written a little note. It said,' Kimmy's jam tarts with fresh cream.' *Alice* said to *Alfie*, "Quick, go and get a pen over there on that table," and *Alice* wrote:

Magic windmill delights
made by *Alice, Alfie* *and friends*

The people at the competition spent all morning looking at the cakes and pies and were amazed by the windmill delights. The afternoon arrived and the whole village was there, mice and all. Mr. Owl and Mr. Mole had dug a hole. They sat under the table with all the other animals.

The place was packed and later the prizes were being presented. The third prize went to Mr. Baker and his mince pies. He was lucky to get a prize because the blackbirds had eaten all his steak pies, leaving just one mince pie. Second prize went to Jacques' friend Kimmy for her lovely jam tarts with fresh cream.

The crowd went quiet and then someone called out "Who is the winner?" The judge said the first prize goes to the village windmill. Jacques came first for his fruit cakes. He stood and rolled his eyes, thinking I never made those fruit cakes. However he still went up to collect his prize, one lovely silver cup and a large box of chocolates. He said, "Thank you so much, I don't know what to say, I must have dreamt. I made them the other day."

Jacques drove home and sat in front of the roaring log fire and he said, "Thank you magic windmill for letting me win the cake competition on the village green."

Alice and *Alfie* thought it was great to see the silver cup above the fireplace and *Alfie* said, "I would love to make a mess in the kitchen another day."
"Another day maybe," replied *Alice*, "but now it is time for bed."

As they went off to sleep, the stars were shining bright and the moon whispered, "Nichole said sleep tight and let tomorrow be just as bright."

Alice and *Alfie* The School Trip

Alice woke *Alfie* and said, "Quick, quick, Jacques is going to the village to deliver some flour to the baker." *Alfie* replied, "Let's go with him and spend some time in the village."

They climbed down the ladder, ran to the barn, leapt into the back of Jacques' van and then jumped into the bucket they always sat in.

Jacques backed the van up to the mill and started loading the flour bags. The wind was blowing and the sails of the windmill were going round and round. He got into the van and off they went. As Jacques drove down the road and through the woods, Mr. Owl flew past crying "to-wit-ta-woo,"
Alice called back, "Twit to you too!"

They reached the village bakery and Jacques got out of the van and went to have some breakfast at a café.
Alice and *Alfie* jumped out of the back of his van and sat at the bus stop watching as the village came alive.

The rag dolls watched the postmaster at the post office and the village policeman, who was saying hello to everybody. *Alice* turned to *Alfie* and said, "Look across the road. There is a library. They ran up to the window and could see it was full of books. The rag dolls crept inside and started looking at all the lovely books. *Alice* kept talking to *Alfie* and the librarian kept telling them to sssh and be quiet. *Alfie* said, "That man is very rude. I think we should leave." and with that they went back across the road to the bus stop.

As they sat at the bus stop they heard children's voices coming from around the corner. As the children came into sight, the rag dolls fell to the floor. A little girl whose name was Michelle saw them and picked them both up and cried, "Wow! They're mine." All her friends hurried to her and said they liked her two new friends and so she put them into her school bag and waited for the bus to arrive.

So *Alice* and *Alfie* were off to school. They peeked out of the top of the bag and as the bus came to a halt, they saw the school. The children got off the bus and went to their classrooms. The little girl took the rag dolls to her first lesson which was English. *Alice* listened to the teacher but *Alfie* was fast asleep in the warm bag. Later they were taken to the next lesson which was maths. The little girl kept telling the rag dolls that when she got home she was going to show them to all her friends. *Alice* just looked at *Alfie* and winked. Sometime later the bell rang and all the children went outside for their playtime. The little girl popped her bag into her desk. It was very dark in there and *Alice* was frightened.

Alfie very slowly pushed open the desk lid. They both looked around and seeing nobody was there they jumped out. In front of them there was a big blackboard with white sticks of chalk lying on a ledge. The two rag dolls began drawing on the board. *Alfie* drew the windmill and the ducks on the river whilst *Alice* wrote a message to all the children in the school. 'Have a good day and be very cool because learning is the only rule.'

Just as they had finished the school bell went 'rrrrinngggg! so they jumped back into the desk before the girls and boys returned moments later. The children came running back into the classroom. They were making so much noise but had to calm down when their teacher came in. The young man stared at the blackboard and said, "Who did all this drawing and writing?" The children all sat there looking at the blackboard and nobody answered him. The teacher told them that he would award a gold star to the child who had done this work as it was very good. The whole class shouted together, "It was me! It was me!" The teacher knew it wasn't all of them, so he said to them I want you all to draw me a windmill and write me a story and the best one will get the gold star.

Inside the desk *Alice* and *Alfie* laughed and laughed, because they could hear what was happening. The little girl was finding it difficult to draw a windmill, let alone write a story. She was so upset she asked the teacher if she could go to the toilet. *Alice* quickly drew the windmill again and *Alfie* made up a short story and slipped it onto the desk. When the little girl came back, there on her desk was the windmill drawing and the story too.

At that moment the teacher walked around the
classroom and collected all the drawings and stories.
He sat at his desk and looked at them all and it was
Alice and *Alfie's* drawing and story that won the gold
star. The little girl could not believe it, but she didn't
say anything. Then the bell rang for dinner break.
The classroom was empty again and *Alice* and *Alfie*
climbed out of the desk.

The rag dolls sat at the window and watched the children playing in the school playground. The girls were playing hopscotch, jumping and singing, and the boys were playing football. Some other boys and girls were playing tag, where they had to run away from each other and then one child had to run and catch them.

The games were fun but not for *Alice* and *Alfie*, they could only watch.

The bell rang again and all the children ran back to their classrooms. *Alice* and *Alfie* didn't have time to go back to Michelle's desk, so they jumped into the nearest one. When Michelle returned and found that the rag dolls had gone she cried and cried. The teacher told her that she should not have bought the rag dolls into the classroom, so it was her own fault for losing them.

The bell rang for the end of the day. All the children took their school bags out of their desks and all went to catch the school bus, except for one little girl whose name was Danielle; her bag was the one *Alice* and *Alfie* had jumped into.

The little girl stood outside the school gate and *Alfie* whispered to *Alice*, "I don't know where we are going to end up." Then along came an old van and driving it was Jacques' friend the baker. He said to Danielle, "Have you had a good day?"
Danielle replied, "Yes, daddy."
He said, "We have got to go a different way home tonight and call into the windmill because I need some more flour to make some more bread." So off they went.

The baker and his daughter drove back to the windmill and went inside to see Jacques. *Alice* and *Alfie* quickly jumped out of the van and ran round to the back of the windmill, up the ladder and into their bedroom. They sat on the windowsill and *Alfie* said, "What luck! That little girl was the baker's daughter," *Alice* replied, "Lucky, lucky, lucky."

The rag dolls went off to sleep and that night the moon shone down on the windmill. He tapped on the window, "How was school today? I saw you having fun and next time I would like to come." he said. "Nichole's star is shining bright, so you both have sweet dreams tonight."

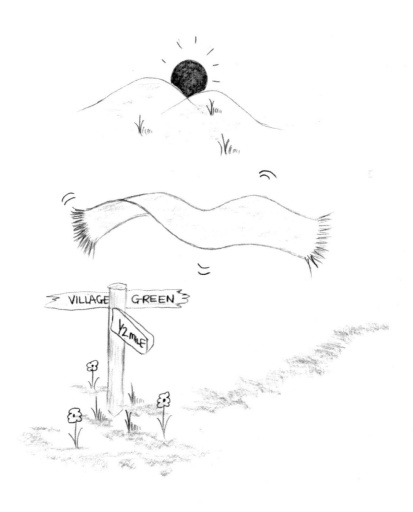

Alice and *Alfie* and the Magic Carpet

Jacques was downstairs having his breakfast when there was a knock at the door. He opened the door and to his surprise it was his sister, Chantal. She said, "It's that time of year again, Jacques, I have come to do the spring clean."
Jacques answered, "Yes, it does need doing."

Chantal sat in the kitchen and Jacques made her a cup of coffee. She told him, "I have come to stay for a couple of days, if that is O.K." Jacques replied, "Of course you can stay. I will be out of your way as I am going to be busy in the mill today. The bakery has put in an extra order for flour. They are making hot cross buns for Easter and extra bread for the village market."

Chantal went upstairs with her bag and put it on the bed. She went across to the open window and saw *Alice* and *Alfie* lying on the windowsill. She picked them up and told them, "I think I will have to clean you two as well." She then went back downstairs to start the cleaning. *Alice* looked at *Alfie* and said, "Do you think we need cleaning?"

Alfie stared at *Alice* and replied, "We are a little bit grubby."

Chantal started cleaning in the kitchen. She polished the furniture, and hoovered the floor and then she went up the stairs. She walked into the bedroom and said, "Now what's for the washing machine? The bed linen, the curtains and while I'm at it I will put the rag dolls in as well."

Chantal went downstairs and threw everything into the washing machine. Chantal switched it on and the motor whirred and the drum began to go round and round.

Alfie and *Alice* found that they were being knocked around all over the place and their faces were right up against the door.

In the corner of the room sat the two mice laughing and laughing. One said, "Look at *Alice* and *Alfie* in the washing machine, we will watch them go round and they will come out clean."
Alice was not enjoying the washing machine and started shouting, "You little mice, let us out," but the mice couldn't help because Chantal was still cleaning in the kitchen.

At last the washing machine finished. Chantal took everything out and pegged it on the washing line. *Alfie* was pegged up by his ears and *Alice* was pegged up by her feet. It was so funny; the rag dolls were swaying from side to side in the wind. Next was the carpet. Chantal pegged it up and the mice ran out and looked up and called, "*Alice* and *Alfie* on the line, they have been washed and they look just fine." *Alice* said, "Stop mice-ing around and get us down."

The mice jumped up onto the line to rescue *Alice* and *Alfie*. It was still swaying from side to side, when all of a sudden the line snapped and they all came tumbling down to the ground.

Alice and *Alfie* landed on the carpet with the mice underneath. At last the mice managed to crawl out and they just sat there with *Alice* and *Alfie*.

Out of the blue flew Mr. Owl who said, "Oh no, no, no, not the magic carpet again!"

"Last year when it was cleaned it caused havoc." Mr. Owl continued flying around the woods and knocking all the trees and shaking all the nests and the eggs. *Alice* enquired, "A carpet that flies?" *Alfie* said, "It must be all lies."

The owl told them that he didn't tell lies and he would say the magic words and they would not believe their eyes. He sat with them on the carpet and said, "Carpet carpet fly for me, around the village green, and over the hills beyond to see what we can see."

Alice said, "I can feel it." It started to move and up they went over the trees and along the river. They saw the castle, but not the wooden prince.

Within minutes they arrived at the village green where the market was in full swing. There were stalls of food including fruit, vegetables and bread and they also saw Jacques with his friend Kimmy.

The magic carpet floated to the ground and the mice ran over to a cake stall and grabbed a strawberry each, with thick cream on top. Mr. and Mrs. Owl swooped down to the bread stall and frightened the stall holders. Mr. Owl grabbed a current bun and flew off towards the sun. *Alice* and *Alfie* just watched and waited for them to come back. When they were full they all came back and off the carpet flew again. It went up up and away.

The magic carpet took them to the bowls club on the village green, a place they had never been to. They landed on the grass and watched the men and women with their white clothes rolling the balls from one end of the grass to the other. Mr. Owl told them that the idea was that they had to hit the jack. *Alice* said, "That is not nice trying to hit Jack."
Mr. Owl replied, "No, it is a small wooden ball which they have to try and hit."

BOWLS MAT

The carpet took off again. It flew across the river and back to the magic garden. It went round and round above the garden and they could see the cricket with the wicket and the rabbits eating the vegetables.

The carpet flew back down to the washing line. *Alfie* tied the line together and the mice hung them back up exactly how they were: *Alfie* by his ears and *Alice* by her feet.

Chantal returned later that evening looked at the two rag dolls and said, "They look clean and dry I will take them in."

Alice and *Alfie* were put back upstairs on the windowsill and the magic carpet was laid back in front of the fire. *Alice* and *Alfie* fell fast asleep. Later the moon shone down and went tap, tap on the window and he said, "I see you were on the magic carpet and it took you to the village market you look very clean. Where have you been?"

Alfie said, "We have been in the washing machine, round and round it went, I thought we would come out bent." The moon giggled and wished them goodnight and sent a loving kiss from Nichole's star shining bright.

"*Alfie*, the rug is a real flyer!"

Alice and *Alfie* A day at the Golf Club

Alice and *Alfie* were fast asleep when they were awoken by their early morning alarm clock. It was the sound of the cock-a-doodle-do. The cock-a-doodle-do kept going on and on and on until Jacques went outside and told him to be quiet. He had woken everybody up: the cats, the mice and also the chickens.

Jacques phoned his friend Francois and said, "Let's go and have a round of golf!" The rag dolls saw Jacques go out to the barn and come back with a bag full of some long wooden sticks with flat rounded heads. He put them in the back of his van. *Alice* had heard the phone call and asked *Alfie*, "Can we go too?" The mice had also heard Jacques and they decided to go and join the rag dolls. The mice went off squeaking all the way to the van.

Alice and *Alfie* climbed down the ladder at the side of the window and by the time they got to the barn Jacques was already in the van. As he drove away, they saw the mice waving from the bucket. They squeaked and squeaked and shouted, "We will meet you at the golf course; you will have to run of course."

The wind was blowing and the sails of the windmill were going woosh, woosh, woosh. Mr. Owl was having fun he was riding round on the hands shouting "Where is that cock-a-doodle-do? He woke me up today and I bet he woke you too."

Alice and Alfie started walking down the lane. Mr. Owl flew down and Alice told him about the mice and that they were going to the golf course.

Mr. Owl said it is a long way but we must find the mice as they might get eaten by Mr. Fox. The owl flew slowly so that *Alice* and *Alfie* could follow.

It started to rain so they stood under some trees until it stopped. As they walked on, the rain dripped down from the trees and hit them on their heads. *Alfie* said, " It's another wet day, a bit like being inside the washing machine yesterday."

Alice replied, "It's only rain, so don't be a pain."

Mr. Owl disappeared into the woods to try and find the mice while *Alice* and *Alfie* walked towards the golf course but there was still no sign of them. They stopped again and had a rest. *Alfie* heard a noise coming from the next tree, so they went over to have a look. There was Mr. Frog sat looking at a book, as he turned the pages he kept saying "read it, read it, read it." *Alice* said, "You must have read a lot of books." Mr. Frog said, "Not really, I just say that when I'm happy."

Alice told him about the mice and Mr. Frog said, "We must find them."

Alice replied, "Mr. Fox might eat them. Fox and mice are not good together. That's the way in any weather."

There was a loud bang and a ping, ping and a small white ball came flying through the trees and hit *Alfie* on the head, "Ouch" He said, "How come it is always me?" *Alice* picked the ball up and Mr. Frog told her it was a golf ball. Mr. Frog said, "It has come from the golf course. It is very hard."

Alfie rubbed his head and replied, "You don't have to tell me, I have a big bump on my head."

Alice and *Alfie* said goodbye to Mr. Frog and started to walk towards the area the ball came from.

In a clearing in the woods they saw the most amazing green grass. In the middle of the grass was a pole in a hole with a red flag flying on top. A long way in the distance they spotted some men with the same wooden sticks with flat rounded heads and bags like Jacques had. As they moved closer they could see one of the men was Jacques. He hit the white ball and nearly hit *Alfie* on the head again. *Alice* looked at him and laughed. The men came down to the green grass and one by one hit their balls into the hole.

Alice and *Alfie* could see the next flag pole in the distance, so they quickly ran through the woods before the men could hit their balls again. They sat down and waited for them. All of a sudden the ground started to tremble and out of a heap of soil popped a head. It was a mole. *Alice* said, "Where did you come from?" And the mole replied, "I'm Colin the Mole, from down the hole."

Alfie said, "Watch out there is another ball on it's way." The ball landed on the green, bounced twice and hit *Alfie* on the head; it then bounced back across the green and straight into the hole.

The men were jumping up and down and shouting that
Jacques had got a hole in one. *Alfie* shouted out
"Yes and my head has got a hole in one too!"

Colin the Mole said, "Let's have some fun with them,
hide behind these bushes and watch me." The next man
hit his ball and Colin started digging all the way under
the green and then popped up and grabbed the ball. He
then did the same to the next man. When all the men
reached the green Jacques' ball was the only one there.
So the other two men had to play again, and Colin stole
their balls once more.

Jacques was winning the game of golf and kept saying to himself, "this must be magic". Just then, it began to rain again and the men put up their umbrellas. The rain was bouncing off them and there on the top of the umbrella were the mice. They were sitting there with smiles on their faces knowing that Mr. Fox was on the prowl but that they had tricked him for now.

Jacques came to the last hole, where *Alice* and *Alfie* watched and waited till the balls dropped. Colin the Mole had collected a lot of balls on the way round the golf course. As the men hit their balls onto the green, he rolled the ones he had all over the place. When the men walked onto the green there were so many balls they did not know which was what or who's was who's. They just looked at each other and decided it was a draw between them all.

Alfie said the mole had come out to play and made everybody's day and with fun and games the mole had won the day and they all walked back to the windmill.

Alice and *Alfie* were so tired they fell asleep on the windowsill. The moon shone down but did not wake them. He just left a note saying that he had seen the fun and games on the golf course. The moon whispered, "Keep your friends very close, as they will look after you when you need them most. Nichole's star is shining bright and her thoughts are with you throughout the night."

Alice and *Alfie*
and the Teddy Bear's Picnic

Alice and *Alfie* woke up to a lovely sunny day. They looked out of the window and saw, Jacques the windmill keeper, feeding the ducks on the river. The ducks were going quack, quack, quack and they waddled out of the water and onto the grass bank.

Jacques's friend Billy Nomates arrived. *Alice* said to
Alfie, "That's a funny name!"
Alfie replied, "Perhaps he's got no friends."

 Jacques and Billy went inside to have some breakfast.
Alice said, "What shall we do today?" as they both sat
there twiddling their thumbs.
"Let's go down to the barn and see what we can find
to play with." *Alfie* answered. "Later we can go for a
walk in the woods."
Alice jumped up and down and cried, "Let's."

The rag dolls crept down the ladder at the side of the window and ran across to the barn. They walked inside and *Alice* said to *Alfie*, "Look, there is a ladder going up to the top of the barn. Let's go and see what's up there." So they climbed up and in the corner were lots of boxes. Inside they found toys and some wooden sticks. *Alfie* picked up the sticks and accidentally dropped them and they fell on the floor in a heap. *Alice* said, "Let's see if we can pick them up without touching the other sticks." The game was called pick-up-sticks and they sat and played for ages.

In the next box there were two little blackboards in wooden frames and some white chalks. "Let's do some drawings," said *Alice*. *Alice* drew a picture of the windmill and *Alfie* drew a picture of Jacques and the ducks. It was so funny because Jacques looked like a matchstick man. They couldn't believe it when they rubbed all the chalk off and were able to start again.

Later on they had a look around and found a box in the corner. On the side of the box it said skittles. The rag dolls decided to take it outside and play. As they got to the top of the ladder they saw a book lying on the floor. The title of the book was THE TEDDY BEARS' PICNIC. *Alice* opened it at the first page and said to *Alfie*, "It says here that if you go down in the woods today you'd better beware as the grey teddy bears are having a party, so you better come dressed smartly."

Alice said, "Can we go *Alfie?*"
"Yes let's." he answered.

The rag dolls picked up the box of skittles and climbed down the ladder. Poking out of an old boot there were two butterfly nets so they took them as well. The rag dolls got outside and started walking down the riverbank. *Alice* said, "How are we going to find the teddy bears' picnic?"

Alfie thought for a moment then replied, "We will have to keep walking and listening until we find them."

It started to get cloudy and *Alfie* said, "It looks like rain."

Alice said, "I do hope there is going to be another rainbow." Then from behind a rock Mr. Frog jumped out and said, "Yes I think it is going to rain cats and dogs."

Alice said, "We had better take cover or they will hurt when they fall on us."

Mr. Frog replied, "Don't worry it is just a saying."

Alfie asked, "What is that hissing noise?"

Mr. Frog announced, "I'm going in a shake. That sounds like Mr. Snake and he is hissing for his dinner. He likes frog pie so I'm off, goodbye." As Mr. Frog hopped off into the woods Mr. Snake went hiss, hiss, hiss. *Alice* looked at him and said, "How long are you?" The snake hissed, "I don't know. I have never seen the end of me."

Alfie commented, "You are as long as you feel." Mr. Snake told them he was looking for frogs. *Alice* said, "Frogs are nice but not to eat. Why not eat fruit: now that's a treat."

Alfie said, "Mr. Snake, we are looking for the teddy bears' picnic. Do you know where it is?"

"Yes, I've just eaten them.......... but don't worry I am only joking." replied Mr. Snake. He told them the teddy bears live in the woods up in the mountains.

"Why don't you jump on my back and I will slither you there."

Mr. Snake went from side to side and up and down. "Hang on," shouted *Alice*, "*Alfie,* have you got the skittles?"

"Yes" he replied, "they're tied to the other end of Mr. Snake."

Mr. Snake slithered through the woods and soon they came to a big waterfall. It was beautiful; clear water was falling from the rocks above and running into a pool at the bottom, where some children were playing. Mr. Snake slithered round the waterfall and back down through the woods where he slithered to a halt.

"Why have we stopped?" asked *Alfie*.

Mr. Snake replied, "Look down there. The teddy bears are having their picnic. I will leave you to it whilst I go back and find some frogs for my tea."

The rag dolls said goodbye and they trotted down
the steps to the five teddy bears who were sitting on
deckchairs eating honey cakes.

Alice said, "Hello, our names are *Alice* and *Alfie*.
Who are you?" The large bear told them that he was
Daddy Bear and the others were Mummy and Baby
Bear and their friends Betty Bear and Fruitie Bear.
Alfie said, "So many bears."

Mummy bear said, "Sit down, and help yourself to
some honey cakes."

Alice and *Alfie* ate the honey cakes and filled their
tummies. Later *Alfie* said, "We have some games with
us. Would you like to play?"
"Yes please," cried the bears.

Alfie set up the skittles and *Alice* gave Mummy Bear
three balls. She threw a ball but it stuck to her hand,
because the honey was sticking to everything. Daddy
Bear said "I know what to do, don't be frightened and
just hold out your hands. He said, "One, two, three let
the bees eat for free."

Just then a dozen bees came flying down from above and landed on their hands and ate all of the honey. *Alfie* said, "Now the games can begin."

The bears and the rag dolls played for a long time until *Alice* said, "We have some nets, shall we go and catch some butterflies?" But the bears had bulging eyes and their tummies were full so they sat down on their chairs and started to feel sleepy.

So *Alice* and *Alfie* said goodbye and wished all the teddies sweet dreams. *Alice* and *Alfie* went back to the windmill. She said, "What a lovely day we have had with the teddy bears. We will have to go again and next time we will take some food." They lay down on the windowsill and went off to sleep.

That night the moon shone down with Nichole's star on his back and said, "sweet dreams, Nichole is not far away and will be back some day".

"*Alfie*, that was a sticky end!"

Alice and *Alfie* The Return of Nichole

It was a warm summer's day and the birds were singing in the trees. *Alice* opened her eyes and saw the sun was shining bright. *Alfie* looked up and said, "Wow, the sun is smiling."

Alice said, "I know, I think it is going to be a special day, there is magic in the air."

 The windmill sails started to turn and they saw the wind blowing them. *Alice* and *Alfie* climbed down the ladder and ran to the river to see what they could see.

Jacques was downstairs having his early morning cup of tea and looking at his silver cup on the shelf over the fireplace. It was the cup he had won at the cake competition. He was so proud of it, even though he didn't know how he had won it. He thought that it was all to do with the magic windmill.

Jacques had just started his breakfast when there was a knock at the door. It was the postman. The postman said, "Just one letter today, Jacques."
"Is it a bill?" asked Jacques.
"Definitely not," the postman replied. "It is a letter from England." Jacques took the letter, said goodbye to the postman and sat down and opened it.

The letter was from Nichole's mummy and daddy, it read, "Jacques, we hope you are keeping well. We will be driving past the windmill in the next couple of days on our way to the South of France." They said they would love to stay for a few days so Nichole could pick up her rag dolls. He phoned them to say that it would be O.K.

Jacques also phoned his friend Kimmy to ask her to
help him clean the mill. Jacques went upstairs but
Alice and *Alfie* weren't there. He looked everywhere
but there was no sign of them. He thought Nichole
would be so sad so he decided to go to town and buy
some new rag dolls for her.

Alice and *Alfie* were playing down on the riverbank.
They saw Jacques driving his van down the lane so they
thought they would go back to the mill and through the
door to the magical garden.

Jacques drove into town and went to a toy shop. He looked around for a long time for new rag dolls but could not find any exactly the same. He decided that the two he found were near enough, so he drove back home and put the new rag dolls back in the box next to the fireplace. Jacques made some flour and baked cakes and bread for the family for when they arrived.

Alice and *Alfie* were having fun in the garden. They were playing a game with Mr. Snake called snakes and ladders. He would climb the ladder and then go hiss, hiss, hiss and then *Alice* and *Alfie* would pull him down again.

The rag dolls watched the hedgehogs. They were rolling around everywhere. *Alfie* picked one up but it was so spiky so he threw it away. It rolled and rolled and knocked over Mr. Mole, who had just popped up for some air. He said, "Ouch, that hurt." and gave Mr. Hedgehog a good telling off.

Alice and Alfie had had a busy day so they went back to the windmill and had an early night. As they dropped off to sleep the moon shone down and said "What a lovely day you have had." He then told them, "Tomorrow is going to be a magical day." And they fell asleep as the moon slipped away.

When they awoke the next morning it was another beautiful day. They heard Jacques whistling and singing to himself. The mice came into the bedroom and said, "Look we have found a book on games and one is called blind man's buff."
Alice asked, "What do we have to do?"
The mice replied, "We tie a piece of cloth over your eyes, then you must try and find us, even though you cannot see. We move around the room and if you touch us the game is over and someone else has a go."
Alice said, "Please, please let us play?"

Alice and *Alfie* did not hear the car coming up the drive to the windmill, nor did they hear the front door open. It was Nichole and her mummy and daddy. Jacques made them some food and drink. Nichole said, "When can I see *Alice* and *Alfie?*" Jacques said straight away." He went over to the fireplace, picked up the box and said to Nichole, "Here you are." She opened the box and wailed "No, no, no. These are not *Alice* and *Alfie.*" and she ran out of the room and up the stairs crying.

Alice, Alfie and the mice were making so much noise they did not hear the door open, *Alice* had the blindfold on whilst *Alfie* and the mice were hiding behind the bed.

Nichole ran into the bedroom and *Alice* grabbed her and shouted "Got you!" *Alice* took off her blindfold and Nichole just fell to the floor in surprise.

Alice just stood there and saw that Nichole now knew for the first time they were not just toys. *Alfie* came out from behind the bed with the mice squeaking away. Nichole jumped with joy and she shouted, "How come you are real?" She then sat on the bed with the rag dolls and told them how much she had missed them. *Alice* sat next to her and told Nichole about all their adventures.

There was a knock on the door it was Nichole's mummy. As she walked in the rag dolls fell limp on the bed. Nichole said, "Look *Alice* and *Alfie* were here all the time." They went back downstairs and Jacques confessed that he had bought two more rag dolls because *Alice* and *Alfie* had gone missing, He told Nichole that he was so pleased she had found them.

That night Nichole went upstairs to bed with *Alice* and *Alfie* as her best friends once again. Before they went to sleep the moon shone down. Nichole opened the window and the moon said, "Hello Nichole, I knew you must be here as your star is nowhere to be seen, only a glow over the magic windmill."

He said, "*Alice* and *Alfie* have come alive, Nichole. You have two little friends for life, so keep them with you all of the time and I would love to come and see you all sometime."

Alice and *Alfie* have come so far keep them safe wherever you are..............

THE END